I0637431

# Scattered Stars:

## The Word Branch Publishing 2016 Science Fiction Anthology

# Scattered Stars:

## The Word Branch Publishing 2016 Science Fiction Anthology

Marble, NC USA
2016

First Edition 2016
Printed in the USA

Cover illustration © 2016 Julian Norwood

Permission can be obtained for re-use of portions of material by writing to the address below.  Some permission requests can be granted free of charge, others carry a fee.

Word Branch Publishing
PO Box 41
Marble, NC  28905

http://wordbranch.com
sales@wordbranch.com

 Library of Congress Control Number:   On file

ISBN-13: 978-0692635179
ISBN-10: 0692635173

Dedicated to Melody Manchester who reached for the stars and is now the brightest shining.

# Acknowledgments

This book couldn't be possible without the dedicated volunteers who made it possible.

Thank you to Kevin Fitch who won the contest to name the anthology with his apt entry: Scattered Stars.

Editors:
- Stacy Bender
- Mara Cunningham
- Bev Guercio
- Brian Goulet
- Jeri Maynard
- Reid Minnich
- Catherine Rayburn-Trobaugh
- Wendy Vogel
- J. Craig Woods

A very special thanks goes out to Julian Norwood for the amazing cover and to Debbi Gehring for her outstanding copy editing.

# Foreword

This third annual anthology is dedicated to the memory of my sister, Melody Manchester, who passed away suddenly in October 2015. One of the last times I saw her was at a Word Branch Publishing book signing in Cincinnati. She was so excited about meeting the authors—especially the science fiction authors. She flitted from table to table introducing herself, getting autographs, and taking pictures. She bought a dragon sculpture made by Stacy Bender and Reid Minnich.

I was so busy that day that I didn't get to spend much time with her, but seeing her unabashed delight is a special memory.

Reading was a sacred obligation in the house my two sisters and I grew up in. Books lined the walls, and every room had ready reading material. Our father read to us nearly every night, and most often it was science fiction. Vision and imagination became ingrained in who we are, and Melody lived this legacy.

I chose the title this year, Scattered Stars, from the excellent entries because it encompassed the idea of this anthology. The stars, the writers, are scattered throughout our world, and they give us their vision through this unique magic of the written word. And from a personal perspective, it gave me hope in my grief that Melody will always be a part of those stars, always shining.

*Catherine Rayburn-Trobaugh*
President: Word Branch Media

# Table of Contents

# Chain Reaction

## By Wendy Vogel

Wendy Vogel is a veterinarian, marathon runner, cancer survivor and SCUBA diver. She lives in Cincinnati with husband Chef Andrew and a houseful of special needs pets. You can find her at www.wendyvogelbooks.com, and follow @drwendyv on Twitter.

~~~

S weat beaded Mya's brow as she pushed the pedals. Just two more miles; you can do it. The only sound in the room was the rhythmic squeaking of the bike chain as she gripped the handlebars and pumped her legs. She leafed through an old magazine perched on the Lucite stand in front of her as the miles flew by.

Done for today. Ten miles. It would do.

She wiped her sweaty neck and padded down the hallway that connected the gym to her apartment complex. The corridor's chilly air cooled her down fast, and she was glad to reach the warmth of her third-floor walkup. The lock clicked behind her.

Her morning bike ride workout routine left her soggy and she indulged in a warm shower, dressing quickly in jeans and a hooded sweatshirt. She poked through the kitchen cupboards to see about breakfast, but the pickings were slim. *Looks like shopping day.*

House keys on a lanyard slipped around her neck. She checked the magazine in the Glock, favorite of her handguns, and tucked it into the back waistband of her jeans. A smaller .22 stayed in the pocket of her winter coat. She shrugged it on, grabbed her backpack, and listened at the door for a moment before opening it and peeking down the hall.

Empty.

On the way down the stairs she paused, remembering that today was Thursday. *Check the water on Thursdays.* She reversed her course and climbed to the fifth story roof access and paused again, listening. No one was ever up there, but it paid to be careful.

Mya lived in the good part of the projects, the newest addition to the city's attempt to clear low income families out of downtown and move them out to the suburbs. The apartment complex was built to modern environmental standards with rooftop rain barrels that supplied about a third of the residents' water needs. It didn't flow out the sinks and wasn't for drinking, but Mya thanked God for it with every hot shower she took.

The barrels were nearly full of gray rainwater as usual. She peered over the roof's edge, scanning the streets around her apartment complex before returning to the staircase and heading down.

At the bottom of the staircase she waited, listening out the door before she pushed it open. Her real bike sat in the alcove under the staircase and she rolled it through the doorway. It locked behind her as she stepped out and her hand reflexively fluttered to her neck where the lanyard of keys hung.

Where to go today? West.

On a hill to the south, she could see the highway as she cycled down the quiet street, and the billboards made her shake her head as always.

DID YOU RIDE TODAY? DO YOUR PART!

The next one said, TOGETHER WE ARE STRONGER! Spray-painted graffiti nearly covered that one.

The next one was a digital billboard and it was blank.

The next one was smaller and more hastily-assembled. It said, MANDATORY VACCINATION 6-15-28. NO EXCLUSIONS.

*Too little, too late,* she thought.

For the brief time that anyone had to agree, everyone agreed that the end of the world had started with the bikes. Ten years ago an enterprising California prison warden got the idea that his prisoners should pull their own environmental weight. He got an engineering firm to cobble together a system where inmates riding stationary bikes in the prison's gymnasium would be hooked into the power grid. Once the bugs were worked out, the prison became energy self-sufficient, completely off California's power supply. Inmates rode in shifts, with hundreds of legs pumping pedals to feed the electric batteries night and day. The warden was in various circles heralded as an innovator, derided as a slave driver, and later, worshiped as a visionary.

Politicians took note. Within two years every city in America had hundreds of spinning stations. They were on the bus lines in the poorest neighborhoods. Want your welfare check? Ride two hours a day to support your city's energy needs. Want your unemployment? Put in your hours on the bike. No legs? No problem. Hand cranked bikes allowed even those with physical disabilities to do their part for society. Liberals loved the supply of clean energy. Conservatives loved seeing all their constituents working for their handouts. Obesity rates among the poor plummeted. And within months, the economies of the middle eastern nations who depended on oil sales fell into ruin.

Mya pedaled down the dusty street, alert for movement. A cold wind chilled her neck and she resolved to look for a scarf today in her shopping. She turned down a likely-looking street and stopped, hiding her bike in the overgrown hedge that was slowly taking over what must have once been a manicured back yard.

She peered in the windows of the house. Dark. No movement. She tried the back door, but it was locked. A decorative garden stone thrown through a first floor window would do just as well. The tinkle of shattering glass echoed across the yard and Mya pressed herself against the back of the house behind the shrubbery, waiting to see if the noise drew any attention.

Nothing.

She crept out from her hiding place and peered around, pistol at her side. She used the gun's barrel to knock out the remaining shards of glass and hoisted herself through the window.

The putrid smell of decaying flesh permeated the house. Mya wished again for a scarf, to cover her nose and mouth as she hunted. She found the source of the smell in the living room. Dead dog. Mya sighed. She hated that. The poor thing had certainly starved to death after the roundups started.

"Sorry, doggie," she said to the dessicated corpse. "None of this shit was your fault." Mya had always liked dogs.

*Do your shopping and get out of here. Time's wastin'*, she reminded herself. She pulled her backpack off and unzipped it. A house with a dead dog in it was a good find. It meant the people who had lived there thought they were coming back. Unless someone else got here first, there would be food.

Mya opened all the kitchen cabinets but found only dishes. The fancy granite countertops were dull with dust and her footprints showed on the tile floor. Two doors led off the kitchen; one probably led to the basement, and the other would be a pantry. She guessed right, and opened a door to reveal a walk-in pantry full of nonperishable food.

*Jackpot.* Canned goods, boxed dry pasta, even two boxes of wrapped granola bars all got stuffed into her backpack. The homeowner had a couple of reusable cloth grocery bags on the pantry shelf, and she filled one with the food that wouldn't fit in her backpack, along with cans of soda and a couple of kids' juice boxes, which might still be drinkable. The load weighed a ton and she heaved the shopping bag over her shoulder, turning for the window.

*Scarf,* she remembered, and set down her haul.

Stepping over the dead dog, she perused the first floor hall closet. Baskets on a shelf labeled "Kadin" and "Kourtney" held child-size mittens and hats in colors indistinguishable in the gray light that spilled in the front window. Rain boots were neatly tucked under the shelf. Mya's throat closed up as she stared into the closet. So little. Two little kids. *Fucking hell.*

A women's down –filled skier's jacket hung next to the smaller children's versions on the rail in the closet. Mya pulled it out and held it up against her own small frame. Warmer than her own jacket, and close enough in size. She pulled the .22 out of her coat's pocket and tucked it into the down coat's, which had a pair of thick wool mittens in the pockets and a heavy scarf tucked into the sleeve. She pulled the coat on and zipped it up. On the way through the living room she laid her old coat over the dead dog as she returned to the kitchen.

Mya reached for her backpack and shopping bag and froze at a noise in the yard. She whipped out the Glock and the .22, crouching under the broken window with her back to the wall.

One heartbeat. Two. Three. *Wait and see.*

After fifty heartbeats of silence, she peeked over the window frame. A family of deer stood in the middle of the backyard, browsing on the remains of what must have once been an herb garden. With a sigh, Mya stuffed her handguns away and picked up her bags. She set them outside the window and crawled through.

The weight of the shopping bag made her bike's rear end sag. The bike was a commuter model with a cargo basket on the back. She'd been lucky to find it early on and it had served her well.

Bikes. It all started with the bikes. The fall of the middle east started a chain reaction. Destabilized governments grew desperate, and it was only a matter of time before one of them went nuclear. Television news showed mushroom cloud after mushroom cloud rising over Pakistan, Israel, Iran and Syria, incinerating millions instantly. Many Americans secretly thought, *good riddance*, as they put on sad expressions for the news cameras. Suicide bombers caused chaos in Europe, but most of the turmoil didn't reach the western hemisphere. When the dust settled, everyone thought it was over.

Mya pedaled through the deserted streets, heading for home. The bike's rear fender scraped against the back tire as she rode, slowing her down, but months of mandatory bike hours before the end of the world had made her legs powerful.

She didn't always live in the projects. At one time she had a house of her own. Nothing like the place she just did her shopping, but a little house in a reasonable neighborhood with her husband and children. She had two daughters and baby James just learning to walk. Her husband worked construction, and everyone said she should have gotten a settlement when the warehouse roof he was working on gave way under his feet, dropping him four stories onto a concrete floor, killing him instantly. But the construction company said it was his own fault. He should have been more careful. Mya lost the house and had to move into the projects. She got a two-bedroom apartment and food stamps, and all she had to do was pedal in the complex's gym four hours a day to help keep the place warm and lit.

Mya remembered blue skies. While the nuclear blasts half a world away hadn't caused the icy nuclear winter the experts on TV feared, they did change the world's climate. Summers were hotter, winters were colder, and the sky was never anything but swirling gray mist. Crops failed and water around the world was tainted, but humanity could survive that. Humans were a tough lot.

She pushed the pedals, sweating in her heavy down coat. The pavement was starting to give way to nature, cracks in the sidewalks and streets buckling as weeds took root and grew in the dim sunlight. Mya swerved to avoid a huge pothole and swore as her overloaded back tire skidded into a crack in the road, popping the tube. The tire flattened and Mya jumped off, assessing the damage. *Dammit.* The rim looked OK. Just needed a new tire tube. She pulled the bikes' emergency pack off its frame and looked inside, but she knew she had replaced the last tube she had a few weeks ago. She'd have to either find a new one, or ditch the bike. *Dammit.*

She hitched the heavy shopping back onto the handlebars and wheeled the bike next to her as she walked. On the way through the neighborhood she had passed a shopping center with a sporting goods store. She hated spending any more time away from the apartment, but keeping the bike moving was worth it. Before the end of the world she'd had no idea how to change a bike tire; now it was a survival skill.

It was hard to tell what time it was without being able to see the sun, but Mya estimated she had enough time to walk the heavily-laden bike to the sporting goods store, get a new tube installed, and pedal home before nightfall. She needed to be safe behind a locked door come nightfall.

Pushing the bike down the middle of the street was risky. But just leaving her apartment was risky, and she had no choice. In the two years since the world ended, all the homes and stores within miles of her apartment had been looted. There was nothing left to eat. She thought of moving; packing up her few belongings and looking for a new place to live. The neighborhood she'd just left was probably full of untouched houses. But without the bike gym for power, there would be no heat . She never turned on any lights at night, fearing the attention a lit window might draw. If she moved out to the suburbs, she'd need fire at night to keep warm. There weren't many left to be drawn to it, but Mya had learned what human contact meant. She rubbed the scar on her upper chest where a bullet still lodged from the last time she encountered her own species. That day she had lost a lot more than blood, and gained more scars than showed on her dark skin. She turned her mind away from the memory.

The sporting goods store was where she remembered it. *Should have raided it long ago.* And it looked like she wasn't the first one to have the idea. The glass doors were shattered, and graffiti adorned the outer walls. She hid the bike and the shopping bag behind the building's air conditioning unit, now heavily overgrown with ivy. The backpack was heavy, but Mya had learned not to leave all her belongings in one place. If someone found the bike and took the food, she wouldn't lose everything.

She drew the Glock and crouched low at the empty doorframe, listening. The store was silent, and would be dark inside. A little penlight was all she dared. She pulled it from the backpack and tucked it into her pocket. Still hunched low, she skittered inside.

Mya had no idea where the bike section would have been. When she'd found her bike abandoned on the street, it already had spare tire tubes in the little pack attached to its frame, along with a small hand pump that took forever to inflate the tires. But she'd used those tubes and now she cursed herself for not replacing them before she needed them. She crept around the perimeter of the store, occasionally shining her penlight ahead.

The hunting section was ransacked. Signs advertising tents, sleeping bags and water bottles hung over empty shelves. The *store wouldn't have carried firearms, but the archery and fishing sections were similarly bare. Wonder who's out there camping? Sitting by the side of some lake with a fishing pole, cooking over a campfire?* She snorted. *Not for long.* Someone would see the fire. And someone with a gun would take the fish from someone with a bow and arrow.

The bike section was largely untouched. Some of the bikes had been knocked over and thrown around, but apparently nobody else thought a bike in the new world was a good idea. The penlight illuminated shelves of cycling accessories; helmets, fancy padded gloves and shorts, mirrors and headlights. She grabbed a full-size bike pump. *Pain in the ass to carry back, but the time it saves will be worth it.* There were baskets of tire tubes arranged by size. Mya didn't know what size the bike she'd found required, so she stuffed five of each size into a tiny backpack that seemed to have a plastic bladder in it for carrying water on long bike rides. Handy.

She retraced her steps and was nearly to the front door when a sharp noise brought her up short. She ducked behind a display of kayaks and hunched over, heart pounding. Maybe just an animal. There were packs of feral dogs everywhere, former house pets and their offspring returned to the wild in the absence of owners long dead. Mya had contributed to those packs in the early days. She broke into every apartment in her complex and let the starving pets run free when it became clear that nobody else was coming home. The place was a lot quieter without their frantic howling. And after the regular food ran out, she knew which apartments were likely to have canned dog and cat food, which didn't taste as bad as she expected.

After a few moments of silence she was about to resume her creep toward the door when she heard it again. There was no mistaking the sound. Quiet footsteps on the tile floor.

*Shit. Shit shit shit.* Almost everybody was dead. Why the hell did some damn survivor have to be in the same damn store at the same damn time?

There weren't many survivors. When the nuclear blasts released their radiation into the air, the water, and the earth, it changed things. People near enough to the sites died fast, of radiation poisoning. Others got sick more slowly, but the scientists all agreed that's where it started, with some sick person who got radiated. It was the worst kind of virus. Some variation on Ebola, pumped up like Godzilla when the radiation changed its DNA. It lay dormant in a person for up to a month before it exploded inside them, and during that month, they infected everyone they came into contact with. By the time the first person broke with it, it was already too late. It was everywhere. The whole world was infected. The NIH made the old Ebola vaccine mandatory, and the American military was dispatched to make sure everybody got the shot in hope of stemming the bloody tide. Whole neighborhoods were rounded up and locked in quarantine. But it didn't work. Inside six months, almost everybody was dead. Some small percentage seemed to be immune to it, including Mya and her oldest daughter Keisha. Keisha's sister and baby James were not. During the roundup when the soldiers came around in their biosuits to take everyone's blood sample, Mya's two youngest children were ripped from her arms, carried screaming away by yellow plastic-clad men with automatic rifles. She didn't know how many survivors there were, because there was no TV news, no internet report to tell her. The power went off and the survivors dug in, desperate people without law or consequence. Bad days.

She huddled on the floor, peeking around the fiberglass boats. Her hand gripped the nearest one as she leaned out, eyes straining in the gray light. Where were they? Was it just one person? Did she have time to bolt out the door?

The kayak gave way without warning and crashed to the ground with a deafening clatter in the silent store. The noise was followed almost immediately by three gunshots.

Shit shit shit. *They're armed.*

Mya eased the large backpack of food and the smaller one with the tire tubes onto the floor. She had slipped the Glock back into her waistband when she was packing up the tubes, and she reached for it now. The .22 rode in her pocket, easy to grab. Mya wished she could shoot with both hands, but if she tried to carry both handguns she was more likely to shoot herself. She kept her left hand on it inside her pocket, ready to whip it out as soon as the Glock was empty.

*They know I'm here. And they know where.*

She scooted away from the overturned kayaks and ran as fast as she could toward the back of the store, ducking low. It got dark fast and she stopped, afraid of crashing into something and giving away her position. With luck, she had gotten behind whoever it was, and they would be silhouetted against the gray light coming in the broken glass doors. She might get a clean shot before they knew she could see them.

Racks of workout clothes were strewn around the floor, and she hopped from one to the other, keeping low. She wasn't sure where the person was in the store, but the gunshots had come from awfully close to where she had been hiding behind the kayaks. If the shooter hadn't bolted when she did, they shouldn't be able to see her.

*Just keep quiet.*

Hand gripped around the Glock and finger on the trigger, she peered around a display of soccer shoes. Movement in the dim light caught her eye and she ducked back behind the shelf. Squinting, she peeked around again.

*Oh, shit. It's a kid.*

Her breath came in ragged gasps. She hadn't gotten much of a look, but it looked like a boy, maybe seven or eight years old. He was waving a pistol around and trying to walk quietly, whipping his head from side to side in near-panic.

She couldn't shoot a kid. She just couldn't. He was her daughter's age.

In the early days she had taken Keisha out looting, looking for food. She hated bringing her eight-year-old along with her, but even with locking doors, Mya couldn't risk leaving the child alone at home. She had heard voices in the hallways a few times, and seen small packs of men outside, walking down the middle of the streets like they owned them.

She held her daughter's hand as they scooted behind their apartment at dusk, searching for a way into the building next door where there might be food or clean water. Mya never saw the men until they grabbed her from behind.

"Well, look here. A mama bear and her little cub, out for a stroll?" The man's breath smelled rotten as he laughed in her ear. He held her arms pinned to her side, and another man held Keisha, wrapping his arms around her small body. A third man aimed a pistol in Mya's direction.

"Don't you touch my girl," Mya whispered. She was outnumbered and unarmed. "You do what you want with me, but you let her go."

"Not sure you're in much of a position to bargain, mama bear. I think I'll do what I want with both of you."

Mya gritted her teeth, praying silently. God, give me strength to save my baby girl.

She relaxed into the man's arms, then shot an elbow back as hard as she could into his ribs when his grip loosened. Her right heel crushed into the top of his foot and he released his arms, clutching his ribs and cursing. The man with the pistol fired, the noise slamming into Mya's ears seconds before her mind registered the pain in her shoulder. He'd shot her.

Her knees crumpled beneath her in shock and she hit the ground hard, sending an electric bolt of agony through her shoulder. The man laughed and pointed the pistol at Keisha's head.

"How about you just stay right there, mama bear. We'll be taking this one with us."

Keisha struggled in the man's grasp and screamed. The man clubbed her in the head with the butt of his pistol. She went silent and limp in his arms, and he tossed her over his shoulder.

Mya struggled to her feet and stumbled after them. She would die before she let them take her child. And she'd rather see Keisha dead than alive in the hands of men like this.

She staggered around the corner in time to see the man toss Keisha into the back of a truck. One man jumped in after her, and the other two climbed into the cab.

"No!" Mya screamed, lunging forward as the truck's engine roared to life.

Casually, the man in the passenger's seat leaned out the window, winked at Mya, and shot her again as the truck sped away.

Mya had crawled back to her apartment and locked herself in, waiting for the bullet wounds to kill her. But the first one had passed straight through the muscle of her shoulder, and the second lodged under her collarbone. As hard as she wished it, she didn't die.

When her strength returned, she ransacked the apartment complex for weapons, finding a cache of handguns and ammunition under someone's bed. She had searched every day for a year, listening for the sound of the truck, looking for any sign of the men who had taken her daughter. She found nothing.

The thought of her little daughter being kept by those men had nearly unhinged her. Every night she looked down the barrels of her handguns as she cleaned them and thought about pulling the trigger. So fast. So easy. No more pain. But a tiny, sane voice insisted from the back of her mind: *If you kill yourself, she'll be theirs forever. You can't find her and save her if she's dead.* Another voice followed: She's probably already dead. As agonizing as the thought was, Mya prayed that the second voice was right.

Now she peeked through the toppled display of running shorts at the boy with the gun. Couldn't be more than eight. He stood only twenty feet from her, holding the pistol in both hands, arms trembling under the weight. It was too dark to see if his finger was on the trigger, but she already knew he would shoot.

*Dammit.*

She should shoot him right now. He couldn't see her, and she could see him, and that made him a sitting duck. Shoot him, take his gun, get the hell out of here.

Mya lifted her Glock and sighted down the barrel.

*Shit shit shit.*

She'd be damned if she'd execute a kid like this. It was probably the stupidest move in history, but she lowered her Glock and spoke quietly.

"Hey, kid. It's OK. I'm coming out, and I'm not going to hurt you."

The kid waved the gun around, searching for the source of the noise. He didn't pull the trigger, which Mya took as a good sign.

She kept her voice quiet and soothing. "I'm going to step out where you can see me. I'm not going to shoot you. I'm not even armed. I just came in here looking for a bike tire, and I don't mean anybody any trouble."

The kid didn't lower the pistol.

Mya tucked the Glock into her pocket for quick access and stepped out into the darkness. The boy whirled to face her, aiming the gun at her midsection. She raised her empty hands in surrender.

"See?" she said. "No gun. Can you lower yours so we can talk?"

The voice inside her head screamed at her. *He's probably not alone. Probably a scout. There's probably a truck full of men outside, idiot.*

The kid lowered the gun but didn't loosen his grip on it. One wrong move and Mya knew he'd fire. Even in the dim light she could see the trembling of his hands on the pistol, aimed at the floor.

"What's your name?"

The boy hesitated, then spoke. "Ryan."

"Hello, Ryan. I'm Mya." She smiled, but he probably couldn't see her expression in the dark. Only her voice could get through to him. "Are you by yourself, Ryan?"

The boy looked toward the shattered door. "No. My dad's with me." But he hesitated too long before he said it, and Mya knew he was lying.

"Okay, Ryan. That's great. I have a daughter about your age. Her name's Keisha." It was the first time Mya said it aloud since the men had tossed her into the truck and skidded away. The name was dry on her tongue.

Ryan didn't answer, but the trembling in his hands relaxed a bit.

"Are you hungry?"

The boy's eyes flashed and his mouth opened a bit. He didn't have to answer.

"I have a lot of food. I'm going to go over there," she pointed to where she'd dropped the backpack, "and get some. Don't shoot me, okay?" She tried to make it sound like a joke.

Keeping her eyes fastened on the boy, she backed through the store, sliding her feet over the dirty tile so she didn't trip. The suddenness of a fall might startle the boy, and if he were startled, he'd likely shoot her before he could even think.

She reached the backpack and crouched over it. Near the top she found three of the wrapped granola bars she'd taken from the house. *Thank you, family, whoever you were, for having granola bars. Canned soup just wouldn't work right now.*

Mya held one of the bars up so the foil wrapper caught the dim light. "You want one?"

Indecision struggled on the boy's face. He was clearly starving. But he didn't trust her. Shouldn't trust her. It was almost two years since the world ended. What had this boy seen in that time? In the end, his stomach overruled his caution and he scuttled over to where Mya squatted on the floor. He grabbed one of the granola bars and set the pistol on the floor next to him so he could use both hands to unwrap the snack and shove it in his mouth.

*Now, Mya. Grab his gun.*

But she didn't. She handed him a second granola bar and one of the juice boxes from the pack. His eyes lit up as he nearly choked on the food.

"How long since you've eaten, Ryan?" she asked.

He drained the juice box and looked at his feet. "Don't remember."

She sighed. "And how long have you been by yourself?"

His mouth opened to protest, then his shoulders sagged. "My dad went out on a food run a month ago. Hasn't come back."

*Sweet mother of God. A month alone in this world.*

16

"Are you from around here?"

"Pretty close." He looked at the backpack and Mya handed him the third granola bar, which he unwrapped and ate more slowly, spitting crumbs as he talked around the mouthfuls. "Dad said if anything ever happened, I should try to get to Aunt Mary in Glenfield."

"Glenfield's a hundred miles away," said Mya. She rummaged in the pack and found a fourth granola bar, which she munched alongside the boy. "How were you going to get there?"

He dropped his eyes. "I thought maybe if I had a bike…"

Mya smiled, her heart breaking at the thought of this lonely boy cycling a hundred miles up the freeway alone.

"Did he talk to Aunt Mary? Are you sure she's there waiting?"

He crumpled the wrapper, then smoothed it out over his knee. "No."

"I see." *Shit. Don't do it. Don't get encumbered. You don't need this.*

Mya ignored the voice. "I'm by myself now, too. But I have a safe place. It's got heat, and power. I can cook all this." She rattled the backpack full of canned goods.

Ryan's eyes darted around the store. "Is…is it far?"

She smiled again, and this time he was close enough to see it. "Not very far. But you will need a bike. Why don't we go back there and pick one out for you?"

He chose a mountain bike that turned out to be blue with white flames once they got it outside into the light. Mya changed her own flat tire, reloaded the bike's basket with the shopping bag of food, and swung her leg over the seat.

Riding side by side, they pedaled together down the empty, silent street, mother and son headed for home.

# The Silver Family

## By M.C. St. John

M.C. St. John is a writer living in Chicago. His works have been published in After Hours Press, Literary Orphans, Maudlin House, Chicago Literati, and Unbroken Journal--the last of which nominated his poem "Telling Stories" for a Pushcart Prize. He is currently working on his first short story collection.

~~~

The scientist Dr. Spencer Kutz arrived at the last house of the twentieth century by sundown. It was a ramshackle old thing, the house, and the purpling sky could be viewed in various veins and holes and soft spots in all of its stories like an autumn leaf pressed against a windowpane. He was alone on the hill with it, standing in awe.

"Look at this," he said. "It's not every day one gets to see the last of the pyramids."

Down in the valley, the glittering circuit board of the new city stretched out to the horizon behind him. If the cataract windows of the old house could see, the doctor thought, the view from its hill would have been one of endless, amazing technological progress. From one neon porthole below he himself had launched in his sleek transit vehicle, zipping down the Mondrian Line highway and leaving a spectral trail of chemicals and light behind. It was only when he reached the edge of the city (who knew there was such a thing? The city was forever, wasn't it?) where there were no magnetized, self-propelled highways but only a road coated with something called ass-fault that the doctor walked, filled with equal parts analysis and wonder. It was uncharted territory, but that hadn't stopped his work for the city engineers—no, uncharted was just another word for unclaimed, in their view.

Then the road became a trail rutted with wildflowers and weeds.

And then just dust.

It was in this dust, just before the porch and the tumbleweed rose bushes, Spencer now stood marveling at the antiquity before him. He adjusted his glasses for a better look and, in doing so, also turned on his field data recorder. With the current time and date noted, he proceeded with his investigation.

"To think, people occupied quarters like this one all over old America. Houses—separate houses. And not just this one in particular but thousands of room variations from the standard bed-dining-bath template. Individual rooms for individual functions. Imagine! The tangle of architecture needed to build just one of these houses would have been extraordinary."

He pointed to the roof of rotten shingles and the ornamentation still perched there.

"A cupola!" he said. "What in the name of efficiency is such a ridiculous structure? How many millions of cupolas were constructed at one point or another for the sake of looking regal? Of looking stylish? And on top of them are what the historical records call a whether-in-vain? I should think so. The damned iron thing just spins and spins, pointing out useless wind patterns." Spencer shook his head, bemused. "There are reasons why certain cultures become extinct. They lull themselves with their whether-in-vains telling them the wind is at their backs…all the way to oblivion." He sniffed. "You, house, are the final gravestone of a world gone by. A fossil to be studied. Congratulations on your survival for science."

Spencer opened his silver valise and produced a large glass jar. Inside were silver ball bearings, no bigger than cat's eye marbles, filling every space within. He unscrewed the top and heard a warm humming. The small robots were waking up, cracking out of their round casings like larvae, and spreading their mechanical wings.

"Initiate housewarming directive," Spencer said to the jar.

The robots heeded their command and flew out in a buzzing wave like silver locusts. Hundreds of them scattered into the night air and organized themselves in squadrons. They attached themselves to the old clapboard sides of the house. Their metal bodies winked and flashed from the basement windows to the tiptop of the cupola. In the gloom, the infestation glittered as if the house were receiving its first winter frost. But then the mandibles of the robots activated and their lasers began slicing.

Spencer watched as the house peeled back, layer by layer, like a rotten artichoke, the petals of which were lifted off by the locusts.

The front door floated by on the flight of a thousand flitting wings and set in the dirt. The robots crawled over the surface, eating away at it, digging in. After a moment, Spencer heard the string of analytics from each insect as it dined on the door:

"Compositional analysis: oak door, aged five-hundred and seventeen years, possible material origins to be statistically found in…"

"…Tudor-style door pattern suggesting an early American domicile of the early twentieth century…"

"…historical fingerprint analysis suggests the last generation to be a family of four…the generation before a family of seven…the generation before…"

And on and on.

Window frames flew by. A length of rain gutter was pulled off like the rib of a corpse. The porch was dissected floorboard by floorboard. A zigzag of stairs landed on the ground, its puzzle pieces disassembled. Armoires were yanked out like rotten teeth.

The anatomy of the house was sliced and laid bare by the insects, the torrents of data points, schematics, and statistics filling Spencer's ears. Overcome by the sheer volume of information, the doctor gave another directive to send the data to the computer in his valise. In this new relative silence, he watched the house being stripped to ruins, his fore-head crinkled and his eyebrows knit together.

"It'll take years to process all of this research," he said. "But to think, a scientist several cycles from me now will see the sets of data line up in a new way and understand a little more about the madness of those early humans. What possessed them to live in personalized asylums with their families? Why did they go through that torture? To what end?"

A white whale of a bathtub sailed out of the disappearing second floor, locusts clinging like silverfish to the surface. Copper and lead pipes followed, dragging toilets, sinks, and faucets. The locusts then carried a vanity mirror, and the oval piece of glass watched the house vanish with an eye fogged with age.

Spencer grimaced at the bathroom pieces. "What filthy things the humans used to clean themselves. What audacity! They kept their toy-lets as heirlooms to fester and rot for the next of kin. Blech." He turned away to hold his gorge.

The locusts continued feeding on the house. There was less and less of it to break down and lift off, and the locusts multiplied to snatch up what remained, faster and faster. The carpets were ripped up, yards of mullioned fabric, and the brass carpet runners tinkled together like a lost wind chime. Parlor furniture flew out of the house with the locusts so thick it looked as though the wingback chairs and ottomans were dipped in living mercury. The façade to the front of the house slid away and there was only the barren stage of the first floor, scarred from years of footsteps and furniture scratches and carpet nails. Then even those were filled in with the silver flow of the robots, a perfect reflecting pool of the dark sky above. The floor began to sag as the locusts ate through.

To calm himself, Spencer switched on the audio feed, lulled by the chorus of analytics again:

"…Current total nail count at five hundred thousand, eight hundred and seventy-three…main metal compositions are iron, lead, tin…"

"…Contents of room A-2 of first floor suggests the last occupant to be a human youth, age four months with a margin of error of twelve days…contents are as follows…one bassinette, one rocking chair, three stuffed animals of unknown classification…"

"…three boots for a full male adult, two umbrellas, sixteen coffee mugs, four spoons, eight serving plates…"

Spencer sighed. His head cleared at the sound of the voices. As he watched the locusts work, he saw the first floor eaten away to the darkness of the cellar below. His robots were efficient. They pulled steamer trunks up by silver towlines, which were then opened to spill out rotted furs, old photographs, and trinkets, and then even those were consumed in silver, transfiguring from solid things in the world to numbers and lists of chemicals for the databanks.

He stood up, the wave of nausea gone, saying, "Better. The numbers are real. Solid. But I still don't understand their sums." He waved his hands at the silver puddles in the dirt drying up to nothing. "These were all things that comprised the house, but aside from that, do they add up to something? A machine is a system of moving parts that can be cataloged, broken down, and re-assembled. Is that what these homes were for these people? A machine to live inside, happy to polish the silverware and decorate the porticos? Change the cooking oil? Reconfigure with new fashions?"

He was still pondering aloud when the last three boxes were hauled out of the hole in the earth. They were larger than the other steamer trunks from the cellar. All of the locusts clung to them, and as they raised the long trunks, they were as pale and shining as shards of bone ripped from an open wound.

The locusts said, "…Compositional analysis reveals one-hundred percent pine wood boards…"

"…Mitered edges reveal early carpentry skills from early Twentieth-century…"

They ate and ate until the boxes were gone.

"…Inner compositional analysis reveals…"

Spencer didn't need the robots to tell him. In the night sky it was easy to see. It was a sky so dark without the electric lights of the new city that the three silver corpses writhing in the air were new monstrous constellations. They were the only things he could see—he couldn't unsee them if he tried.

Two of the bodies were adults, a man and woman. They jerked and shook above Spencer, their long limbs propelled by the flitting of their now silver skin, the locusts boring into dead flesh, galvanizing what the damp earth had not yet moldered.

The locusts said, "…Female specimen, aged twenty-six with a margin of error of eight days, genetic code isolates hereditary information to the following areas…."

"...Pockets of deceased male contain one pocket watch, gold-plated at the following percentages...also one ring, gold, with the inscription..."

Spencer wasn't listening to the murmur of their information. He was too busy cowering back and away from the third floating corpse—a child swaddled in rotted cloth. It hung above him as a titanium-colored cocoon, much like an enlarged casing for one of the locusts. The only difference being that Spencer could see the hollows of the child's eyes, black holes in the silver crawling skin, and no matter where the doctor moved, those sockets pinned him in their stare.

"Stop," he said. "Please stop, don't come any—" He tripped over his own valise and stumbled into the dirt. Flat on his back, he watched the silver bodies as a boy would watch clouds, guessing what shapes they were. Spencer knew the shapes above him—they were the shapes of nightmares. The man and woman corpses twirled down to the ground with soft thumps. He whimpered, still watching the child float down.

"...third specimen is a female infant, aged..."

The swaddle had vanished, been eaten away, and now Spencer only saw the child's bones, her poor bones, spinning like a dandelion gone to seed, coming ever closer to the ground. He dug his heels into the dirt and scooted back on his elbows, his skin slick with cold sweat, his glasses askew. "Computer, cease Housewarming Directive," he said.

Somewhere, his valise answered, "Please repeat initiative."

Spencer swallowed, tried to still his heart and steady his voice, and said, "Cease. Housewarming. Direct—eh! Eh, eh, eh..."

What remained of the child landed without a sound on Spencer's leg. He felt the vibrations of the little locusts eating away at the skull, whose silver jaw rested just below the knee, the hollowed eyes fixed on him. The small hands, what was left of them, clung to his calf. Spencer cried out again.

"Please repeat initiative," the valise said.

"Cease Housewarming Initiative now!"

The chorus of murmurs ceased into a dying drone. The locusts deactivated, folding in their mechanical wings and rolling their bodies into tight spheres, which rolled through the dirt like drops of mercury towards the valise, towards their glass jar.

Spencer watched as the sheen of quicksilver slid away from the child's bones. He had enough courage to slide his leg out from the grasp of those little fingers, away from the depthless stare of those little eyes. Without the robots covering her, the child was nothing but a dried husk the color of November. She rustled as he moved away.

The doctor found himself at the edge of the hole where the house once stood. He also found himself crying, soft and frightened, at what just happened. No one from the laboratory and the city knew he was here. Without the merry hum of his robots, he realized for the first time that he was quite alone. No, not alone—there were the bodies…the child…

He tapped his glasses and said, "Computer, contact Chief Engineer Jones of my coordinates for reconnaissance."

"Searching for coordinates," the valise said. "Please hold."

"Hurry," he said.

Night was coming to the hill, the shades of twilight laying darker layers around the doctor. It was getting harder to see the valise lying only a dozen feet away, whirring away, calculating coordinates. The time stretched out as Spencer waited for word, any word, from the glowing geometry of the city, which was so far away from the doctor that he wondered if it wasn't just a toy model. A model for a child while growing up and…

"It was a mistake coming here. The house should have just stayed the way it was." Spencer looked into the gloom and said to them, "I'm sorry

I came. You all don't have a place. There are no more places like this now. The parts are all gone." He lowered his voice. "All of your parts are all gone." He closed his eyes. "Computer, please hurry…"

Whatever the doctor wanted to say next dried up in his throat. There was a shuffling in the dust, twigs writing cursive in the dark. He held his breath. He forced his eyes open, one after the other, and looked into the shadows.

Two figures had reared up nearby. At first, Spencer believe there were still some of the locusts clinging to the mother and father, for their skin was silver in the darkness. But the color was not the glaring metal of the robots. It was a soft silver, worn as cobwebs. And within those sheaths of silk and gossamer the doctor saw the sets of old worn bones, what was left of them, ribcages and collarbones, a pair of hips, a skull, a xylophone of spine, shuffling through the dirt towards him. He couldn't speak, couldn't move.

This is what I deserve, he thought. Numbers won't save me now. It's as if I killed them all over again.

Closer and closer they came. The mother was the first to arrive almost at Spencer's feet. He saw her hair, silver and floating, around a skull missing its jawbone. She considered him for a moment before she bent down towards him, close enough so he could smell the dried honeycombs of her marrow, and he braced for her hands to wrap around his throat…

And then she lifted her daughter up from the dirt.

The little girl was a grinning skull and ribcage, but her unblemished skin held her bones like strands of silk. She was crying without a sound. Aside from the clacking of her small bones, there was silence.

The father joined them, mostly a lower set of legs traipsing up to his wife and daughter. He touched his wife's shoulders with silver hands, and then he surveyed the maw in the earth where the house once stood.

Watching the three of them stand there, the doctor thought of the archives back in the city and the few phoddy-graphs in the historical collection. Many early human families stood like that before their houses, some smiling and holding each other, as if those structures of wood and carpet and glass were the whole point of living. Perhaps they were for those humans, which was the logical conclusion, the most straightforward answer.

Or maybe—just maybe—there was something more to the house, something between the people, inside their gears, really running and propelling the machine. After all, a heart needed blood to circulate. Otherwise it was only a useless muscle…

The woman held her baby tight, shushing her with a sound that may have been a breeze through the dust. The baby calmed down, and her skull gazed up at her mother with a calm wonder. She was back where she belonged, back in her mother's arms. They had all been disturbed from their long peaceful sleep, but now the excitement was over. It was time to go back to bed.

The father was the first to climb down the steep embankment that was once their cellar. His foot bones made scraping noises into the earth, pitchfork and spade noises, shifting dirt. He held his wife's ribs steady as she waddled down the slope too. Her balance was important because she held the baby girl in her silver arms and old bones. The last thing she would have wanted to do was lose her again.

The child peeked out from over her mother's shoulder. She was growing tired, Spencer could see, but her opal eyes were wide and bright. They drank in the glowing city in the valley behind him, its straight neon lines and burning glass spheres, and the doctor imagined the sight for that little girl would have been a fantastic dream.

And when the silver family disappeared underground, Spencer wondered if what he just saw was a dream as well. His eyes were wide behind his glasses, the air thick inside his lungs. The stars above him were doubling and tripling in his vision. His head felt very light. He knew the signs of a fainting spell.

A click and hum finally came from the valise. "Coordinates successfully routed to Chief Engineer Jones. Connecting." Spencer heard the words, but his mind was elsewhere.

There's something more to these houses and their humans, Spencer thought, but the only proof I have is what I saw. What I felt.

Then a new voice piped out of the valise. "Kutz, it's Jones. Do you read me?"

Spencer groaned.

"Are these coordinates correct? What are you doing outside of the grid? In fact, never mind. I want an explanation recorded in engineering script to verify your intentions and actions on this nonsensical venture of yours into the hinterlands. Upon review, I will determine if I should strip you of your scientist ranking. You have been as much reckless as methodical with your compulsions to know…"

Chief Engineer Jones went on and on, each word becoming more fuzzy than the last in Spencer's ear. The doctor paid no mind.

At the edge of the hole, there was only darkness. But in that darkness, he felt the presence of the family, the warmth of them, a feeling that the locusts could never detect and measure and assign a number. There was something beautiful about that—humbling too. There are ghosts in the machine, he thought with a wonder. And they are in love.

"…Kutz, do you hear me? I've sent an air-transit unit to pick you up. But you just tell me now, before you put it in the report—what the hell were you looking for out there?"

Smiling in the dark, he said, "A home."

"A what?"

"The address is 32 Evergreen Terrace, and it is lovely…"

Before Spencer fainted, he saw a glimmer of silver deep down in the earth. It was a small and wonderful face looking up at him, a face on the verge of dreaming or waking, warm in an embrace, feeling more of the world around her than seeing ever could. When his own darkness slipped over him, the doctor sensed that face was still somewhere nearby, and the comfort of knowing it in his heart went beyond calculation.

# Tenets in Space

## By Lynn Allen

Lynn Allen was born in Detroit, Michigan and raised in Oakland County. She's been writing prayers, poems and stories since elementary school. She currently lives in Wolverine Lake, MI.

~~~

I woke standing, staring up at a clear, star-studded sky. A high sky. Cold. Filled with star patterns I did not know.

Why did I not want to look down?

Why couldn't I remember where I was or how I had gotten…

"Excuse me, Miss? Could you help me?"

It wasn't a 'living' voice.

Looking in the direction of the voice, I became aware of my new world, a junkyard filled with all things metal, including the machine asking for assistance.

"How can I help you?" The question and my steps seemed slow, as if I were drugged or recovering from a head wound. Could it be an effect of the environment?

"Is something wrong, Miss?"

I didn't know machines could sound concerned. Did I look that bad?

Crouching down before the half buried robot, I noted that it was covered in dirt and an oily substance. The lights that would be eyes were a pale orange color, perhaps because they looked through a film of grime.

"How can I help?" Reaching out to touch it, as if to confirm its presence, the reality of what I was seeing.

It reached out to me, got hold of something not me and pulled, hard. The tug parted something at the back of my neck, I felt a sudden freedom.

And hit the hard ground on my tail.

Tail?

"I am so sorry. Are you alright, Miss?"

It held a disk on a fine chain in one hand, a disk, or rather medallion that I hadn't seen in a very, very long time.

Not since my Master had been sent away for her crimes and I had been set free.

I reached for it, why, I couldn't say. Before I could touch it, the robot crushed it.

"Hey-" I began, then I noticed something not quite right about my hand, my arm; I was covered in fur. Dark brown from finger tips to the elbows and a dark fawn further up, my chest and abdomen a shade lighter.

"It was a slave collar. You will feel better in a moment. I am called Ceil. I am an Emissary android. "

I was only half listening to the machine, looking my furry self over. I'd always been in human-form for my missions. Of course, my messages were mostly for humans.

What was so different about this mission?

I looked up at the robot.

"Emissary? You can identify different species?" I asked, though I had an idea what I was.

"Yes. I am programmed with the languages and customs of many star faring species."

"Good. What am I?" This would be interesting.

"What are you? Are you having a memory problem, Miss?"

"It must be the after effects of the slave collar." I rose to look around. "Well?"

"There are several feline races similar to your form."

"You ever hear of the En'Duri?" I asked. Even if it hadn't, that was what I was going with. I knew the species from a well remembered past.

"Yes. Are you sure? There haven't been any sightings since the Consortium gained mining rights to planets in the M12-80 system almost fifty years ago."

This was not good to hear.

"Where are we?"

"A small planet in a system designated J18-23. It is a planet used for ship disposal and garbage."

It looked as if anything and everything was just dropped off. Ceil had been. I took a closer look at the machine.

"Been through some rough negotiations lately?" I asked, looking about for the missing parts.

"I must have been suffering a systems failure. The two parties who were in negotiations decided I was the problem. Their solution was to tear me apart and throw me out with the trash. I have been here ever since." Can machines sound dejected?

"Some folks only agree with each other over similar dislikes," I said. "Contrary like."

"I should never have taken the assignment." A sigh? Regret?

I started pulling parts of android out of the rubbish, setting it all out in alignment, to make sure I had found everything.

Ceil was very helpful in the location process. It only took about an hour, mostly due to having to track down some parts that had fallen a distance away.

All parts assembled (gathered), now all I needed were the tools to put Ceil back together.

"Got any ideas on where to look?" I asked, having found nothing of use so far.

"I'm sorry, Miss. I have no idea where to look."

Silly me. "Alright, there must be some tools around here somewhere. Don't go wandering off."

...

Why this place wasn't being salvaged I had no idea. With time, tools and a little help from people with the know-how, a lot of these ships could be back in space. Question was, why had they been left here in the first place?

Of course, some had large holes in the hulls. Holes one could fly a smaller ship through. Or were broken in half, like some tree limb, snapped in the middle by a lightning bolt. Insides burnt out, torn out.

Thing was, the damage didn't look all that old. The scorch marks had no dust, the breaks had no rust. The garbage seemed more moved than dumped on them.

Had me wondering why. And, thinking it may have something to do with why I was here in the first place.

Looking up, I noticed that the stars were fading as the sky took on a more ashen tint. The open hull of a huge ship stood before me. Inside the skeletal framework led me up to an opening, the perfect place to watch the sun rise.

Taking a deep breath, I sang my morning ritual song to my patron, The Dawnbringer:

"Without the bird song,

I am the voice that will herald in

The approach of Dawn's first light.

 Let this day begin with sun light.

Chase away the cold night chill,

That I may warm myself in the glow of a new day.

A new day dawns, on a world far from home.

Freedom comes again, a friend in need.

I greet the light of Dawn with joy and song."

She stood before me in her armor of red, yellow and gold, night black hair framed a fair face, ice blue eyes, and her warm, friendly smile, shielding me from the sun.

"Free now on this plane this body is." She embraced me, then, held me at arms' length. "Your true form waits for your return, My Harbinger."

"More than a simple message, then?"

She released me, laughing.

"When has any message ever been 'simple', Horustondis?" She handed me my haversack and a canteen of water.

"True," I agreed, accepting both gratefully. "It may take me a while to leave this clutter. My new instructor is in need of some repair and I'm having one hell of a time finding the tools to repair her."

The Dawnbringer looked about, then, nodded toward a nearby mountain of trash.

"Try the other side of that one. You'll find some help there."

Turning, she took several steps away, then, turned back.

"The rest of your supplies are down below. Along with a few other necessities. The atmosphere is lacking here.

"Why this body?" I asked.

"We will speak on this later. Make your supplies last several days. We are rather busy back home."

Then she was gone.

Below, I ate a little, drank a little, put on the respirator and headed north

…

If beeps and clicks can be called frustrated that is what drew me to Auri.

Buried under what looked like several trash dumps from very large vessels, I took up a good sized pipe and began to dig it out.

It took some time, but I finally got to an upended anti-grav sled that looked as if it had been struck by or passed over, an incendiary round. It looked as if the backend had taken the most damage. With great care, I got the sled onto its side…

The beeping got a bit excited and I stopped what I was doing. Didn't want to damage the machine, so I used my pipe to prop up the sled and looked to see what could be done to do as little damage to the machine as possible.

It was still trapped in trash that needed to be removed, or did it? On moving some good sized blocky bits, I started bracing the sled up until Auri was clear. Crouching down, I looked what I could over.

"Flip you over to the side or back end?" I asked.

It was an odd, low key wail, something I might equate with the knowledge of unavoidable pain.

I'm learning more about machines every minute.

A circle where the base of the robot was attached to the sled turned and came apart suddenly. Then the machine hit the ground dome first, falling full length onto the slightly cleared area below.

Carefully, I pulled it out and onto clear ground, helping it up.

"Are you all right?" I asked, carefully brushing off the dusty lens.

It replied with a happy beep of I translated as affirmative.

"You wouldn't happen to know where we might find some tools? I have an android friend who's gone to pieces."

Several small panels opened to reveal some impressive implements, then returned behind the panels..

"Great. Let's get back to Ceil before she starts to think I've gotten lost or forgot about her."

The beep sounded like a question. Whether my answer was correct or not, Ceil could tell me when we got back.

"The speech pattern makes me think female." I said. "'It' seems...cold. Unless that would be offensive to my friends."

Two beeps and a whistle. The sled rose, a little awkwardly and I got on.

"We'll find the parts to fix that."

On the way back to Ceil we picked up my provisions.

Ceil was very pleased at our return and greeted Auri with enthusiasm. We got on with the repairs right away. I was mostly used to bringing the parts together for Auri to re-attach wires and get the nuts and bolts back into place. Re-weld some metal, which was replaceable from the refuse around us.

Ceil was up and walking after a few hours and some re-adjustment. Good as new.

The sun was huge and hot. I was panting, my palms and foot-pads were sweating. We needed shelter and fast.

Auri led us to the broken out side of a ship. The shadows were deep and little debris was within. We went inside, finding a clear place to curl up and I fell asleep.

...

I had a dream of my past, flashes of what had been: the death of my mother, my father bringing his second wife home. We did get on well. The birth of my half-brother and, on my fourteenth birthday, my father selling me to a high born lady of another race for my dower price.

Once the medallion was around my neck and 'The Word' said, I was hers.

…

I woke with a start. My movement alerted my companions at once.

"Is something wrong, Miss?" Ceil asked, concern in her voice.

"A nightmare." I sat up and stretched. "The slave collar seems to have tapped my past."

"You are free now," Ceil assured me. "What shall I call you?"

"Horustondis Magpie," I said, rising from the ground, starting some stretching exercises.

"But, that is a human name," Ceil observed.

She was right. En'Duri names were usually three to four letters, an apostrophe then rel for females, three to four letters, an apostrophe and either ant or ren for males, depending on their mating records. Queens had offspring, as did Toms. Those who had yet to produce offspring Kitlings until the first litter.

Was I Queen or Kitling?

Whatever, I was Harbinger.

"Will Mag'rel do, Emissary Ceil?" I asked.

"I believe it will, Mag'rel, I am so happy to make your acquaintance."

"It feels as if the sun has set. Let's go out and look for some parts and maybe we'll find some tools. I think I saw a few anti grav sleds that could be used for spare parts. Have a platform to carry our goods on through this maze of stuff.

With replacement parts, we repaired Auri's anti grav sled and put our 'treasures' on it; an old tool box that originally held a single screwdriver, a three foot coil of corrugated metal, left over bits of plastic coated wire, more replacement parts for the sled, a few bits and pieces for the robots.

Auri's light made it easy to look into loose piles of junk. We had to be careful. Metal has sharp bits and we, as of yet, have no first aid kit.

Dawn was making its way around again.

"To sail by sea, The stars you'll see

One motionless rules the night, a guiding light

Moon and Sun move east to west

One star to plot the night."

Each point of light is either a star, planet or asteroid," Ceil explained. "No two views are exactly alike. Over the centuries the stars shift their positions, become bright, dull, go nova and are no more."

"My home is long gone," I said, looking at a broken light fixture, intricate metal work twisted and warped.

We found a trunk with a broken hinge, I could fix that, use it for our treasures.

Dawnbringer had said they were busy.

I missed my things all of the possessions I'd always had with me on my previous missions: sword, axe, bow, daggers, spears.

I suppose the weapons are too old fashion. My art unnecessary or too dangerous.

Or, I just don't need them at the moment.

I stopped more often to look things over, remembering other time, other searches for treasure.

"Ceil, what is going on?" I asked, finding another twisted light fixture, this one looked as if it could have been a chandelier, several crystals lay shattered on the ground. Partially hidden under a broken bit of plate, I found one complete drop.

"Going on? I don't quite understand." She was doing more looking than touching, calling my attention to repair parts, while I was just curious about everything.

The name 'Magpie' fit quite nicely, thank you very much.

"The time you've both spent here, have the drop offs of the ships increased? Some of the hulls we've slept in are not what I'd expect to be dumped without some repair work. Aside from the obvious recent damage…"

Auri gave a long series of low whistles, beeps and other noises that Ceil interpreted.

"Auri had been on a luxury liner, picking up and delivering clean clothing, linen and the like to the exclusive guests. The ship was taken by slavers, the passengers and crew removed and the ship brought here for disposal. The majority of the android staff had been gathered in the storage area above the engine room and were destroyed with the ship. He escaped by being trapped under a pile of laundry when the ship had initially been attacked."

"Break the ship and dump it here, no one would think to look for the wreckage here."

I thought about the passengers and crew. "They would need a ship with a large hold, several, to move that many people. And keep them healthy enough to make a profit."

"Miss Mag'rel, have you done this before?" Ceil sounded aghast.

Part of the programming?

"No. I fought people like that. Not easy when the authorities or the local lord is in cahoots with the slavers." I had a thought. "Auri, do you recall hearing a distress call being sent out at any time?"

The answering whistle was a negative. The list of inquiry was getting longer.

The search for parts was now a search for clues.

…

We searched the broken hulls, looking for clues as to what the vessel had been, before sleeping in the afternoon. Both Ceil and Auri were able to identify all but the oldest or most mangled ships in the junkyard.

I had chosen not to sleep so deep inside that afternoon, using a large piece of corrugated metal as an awning, I watched the shadows shift, slowing falling asleep…

Something deep below the surface was stirring, the faint vibration of power passing through me.

"Ivy?" I asked. The vibration ceased, as if listening for confirmation. "Ivy, I feel you."

The seizing ground; Ceils' cries and Auri's frantic beeps woke me. Our shelter was loosing what little stability it had.

We got out before the entrance was covered in the shifting trash slide.

"Auri epicenter " I was watching for more debris slides. Even the androids could lose limbs if we weren't careful.

The land suddenly became quiet, the last slides shuddered and were still. An odd shift could be heard every so often.

Auri made its report.

"North," Ceil reported, pointing slightly up. "Beyond that."

Ahead of us was the broken hull of a ship that looked as if it was a multi environmental vessel. What looked like the skeletons of towers rose out at various angles, due to the awkward skew of the broken hull.

"Auri, take us to that hull. We'll use it as a lookout post. A base of operation."

"A storage locker?" Ceil suggested.

"For now," I agreed.

…

The derelict that became our base of operation had been here for quite some time. There were many repair welds, rusted areas, many layers of flaking paint. It reminded me of the ship I'd sailed on across the Atlantic Ocean on my second mission to Earth in the mid-1800's:

close quarters, little air circulation, not much in the way of sanitary facilities. Or privacy.

When the children had fallen off to sleep, giving the adults some quiet, you could hear the music from the ballrooms and saloons above, where the elite were. Having their fine food and drink, clean beds and toilets, with clean water to wash with. And clean sea air to breath.

I promised myself, next time, I was going to travel in style.

Auri found us a way inside.

Again, like most ships, it had been gutted of furnishings and fixtures, carpet and paneling. There were gaping holes about the lower portions of the vessel, as if shot through repeatedly below the water line.

A ship of both sea and space. Must have been a spectacular sight at one time.

...

We kept looking for spare parts and clues to the damaged spacecraft. We'd choose a direction in the evening, get a few hours sleep, then go out about midnight so we could move in the coolness of night and search in the moonlight.

My night vision was awesome. Of course, some things are best looked at in the bright sunlight...

One night, amongst some hills of trash we found mounds that seemed to have been targeted. Whatever had been dumped had been blasted to near ash. I'd asked Auri if the damage could have been made by the same weapon that had damaged the ships.

The answer had been yes.

We all looked around the site for anything that might have escaped and Auri found two trunks that seemed to have rolled into hiding.

One was women's clothes, not that I needed any. Inside were the usual foundation garment, gloves, soft foot ware and light colored hooded robes with attached veils. All of a light fabric.

Protection from sun and dust, a layer of warmth in the night.

The second trunk had belonged to a male. The bonus was that he kept his thoughts private in journals.

I now had a way to learn how people actually thought. At least one person.

The woman had had an album, but left no words behind.

We brought it all home.

Later, Auri had sent for me. The lookout spot was set on the highest spot of the old derelict; the remains of the access ladder to the satellite dish,

It's a beautiful view. Scary as hell, that first step.

Auri pointed out our next destination.

...

They were all standing in a circle, nose down, as if thrown into the ground like giant darts. The cargo holds missing their blast doors. Ten feet above the ground, the hulls all had the same blast pattern as the cruise ships.

Auri hovered to the opening and looked inside.

"The interior has been stripped away, similar to the cruise ships," Ceil reported. "Shall he check another?"

"No." I stepped around the ship. The metal was a dark color, almost like old, dried blood.

"Ceil, what type of ship is this? A freighter, I know, but where did it come from? Who pilots them?"

"That would be Range Stalkers. The Saurian Houses use them. The odd color is from the metal of their planet in the system K37-03. "

"Saurian? Reptilian?" I asked.

"No. They have always walked upright," Ceil said. "A warrior race. Family is important. They are a noble race. Clans are ruled by the most powerful House. At my last update, there were only three Houses ruling the Clans."

"War among the Houses?" I left the ship to look at a small pile of debris.

"No. They do not fight amongst themselves. It seems someone is targeting them."

"Any ideas who?" I hadn't found anything of use, so I returned to the anti-grav sled for my personal transportation: an anti-grav board., though, 'board' was a too narrow term, it was shaped more like an arrowhead with an extension in the middle. It could ride two, if they were real friendly.

"There had been no claims made by any before my…dismissal," Ceil said.

"Think they got all the numbers off all the ships?" I asked Ceil as I set the board on a clear patch of ground.

"We would have to find shovels." Ceil reminded me.

When was the last time a shovel was on a starship that wasn't an explorer?

I was about to toe the board to life, when the wind shifted, bringing a stench I knew only too well.

"Miss Mag'rel, what is it?"

"Decomp." I hissed, wishing for a strong, floral scent.

"You mean-someone had died here?" Ceil was shocked.

"Within a ten day." I started the board and followed the stench through the ship circle to the west and down into a depression larger than the one north of our derelict.

On the floor of the depression were bodies in various stages of decay. The first skeletal remains caught my eye; upon the bleached-white bone of the sternum lay a medallion of the same metal as that of the ships in the circle above the depression.

I brought the board down, shut it off then, carefully, approached the bones.

They weren't alone. Hundreds of skeletons lay strewn about.

The not so decayed were further west, north and south.

At the remains, I crouched down, reaching for the medallion, taking in the condition of the bones. Whoever he had been, his life had not been easy. Many of the bones had been broken and healed nicely. There did not appear to be any killing damage, no burnt bones.

Poisoning was not a good way for a warrior to go.

I took up the medallion, disturbing the vertebra, the jaw and the head, all of which rolled and clattered, rather loudly, only a short distance, revealing a fist sized hole in the skull.

Ceil's warning was not as loud as Auri's high pitched shriek, like nails on a chalkboard.

The smell around me had changed, bringing back memories I would much rather have remained buried, thank you very much.

I spun around, looking over the field of the dead and there it was: black and putrid yellow, huge, the near human face rising up on the long, uncoiling, serpentine form. Its many pairs of arms ending in pincers.

Round eyes, like the tops of cut diamonds, a human-like mouth sporting sharp serrated teeth. From the dark opening, a mouthful of pale pink tongues extending with a scream that was terror on its own.

A carrion worm. What the hell was it doing here?

The bodies.

I leapt for the board, got it pointed in the right direction, toed it on and got about three feet into the air when the tail of the monster knocked the board out from under me.

Of course I landed like the cat I was and slid down on a sheet of metal.

Damn.

The ugly thing hovered above me, its drool just missing me.

Bones amongst metal is not the most stable ground.

It drew back, smiling, already anticipating fresh meat..

An orange ray struck it right in the mouth, burning the tongues, angling up into the brain. The heat caused the skull to explode. Almost dropping the thing on me.

The stench was repellant.

The body twitched hugely.

No hesitation. I got up, saw my board and went for it.

The worm went still as I flipped the board over.

I looked back at the body, the yellow underbelly was moving, bulging with wormy looking-

Oh crap, young.

I hit the start button and headed back topside.

Someone was coming down, weapon in arms.

I could say 'fool', but did he even know what it was?

"Get on!" I yelled, slowing, offering my gloved hand.

I watched him looking back. He suddenly paled.

Gun quickly shouldered, he joined me, holding on tight and I sent us quickly up the side.

"Ceil, Auri, Move," I yelled.

Ceil got on the sled as Auri moved out at a pretty good speed.

Multiple shrieks had us both shuddering.

Hopefully they would go for the easy prey and not come after us living.

We wove between the ships and didn't stop until we had at least one derelict and a mountain of trash between us and the killing field.

I stopped my board, landed, shutting it down. My passenger released his grip on me and stepped onto solid ground as Auri stopped the sled next to us.

"Captain Mag'rel," Ceil said. "What was that thing? I have no record of such a creature."

"Carrion Worm," I said, stepping up to the sled and showing him the medallion. "What is it and where's it from?"

Ceil took the object and looked it over.

"This is a Saurian Clan/House medallion. Last update, it was held by the head of one of the last three remaining houses of this particular Clan." She looked at me, her attitude of shock coming through. "This is not good."

"Keep it safe for me." I opened one of the trunks and took off my gloves. We would be going home now and I wanted to not be encumbered by clothing. After the robe was folded and closed away in the trunk, I turned to our guest.

Had I been in my human form, we would have been looking eye to eye. As it was, he was at least six inches taller than I was. His long, auburn hair was tied back, but also bound by a breathing apparatus. Tanned. Blue eyes and a beard.

His expression told me he'd most likely never seen an En'Duri before.

Time to be political.

Right hand to my chest, I bowed to him, in the tradition of the planet my form was from.

"We thank you for the timely rescue from the beast," I said. "I am Horustondis Magpie. My companions are Ceil, an emissary android and Auri, a maintenance android."

"Zack Harrisson. Scout," he said, almost as if he'd just remembered.

"You must have landed after we left the derelict," I said, walking back to my board.

"How do you figure?" he asked, stepping back, keeping us all in sight.

"All the metal blocks signals. We took up residence in a large derelict north and west of here because from it we can see over the highest piles of trash." I stepped onto the board. "Auri stands watch in case anyone comes to dump trash or anything else."

"Where is your ship?" The scout asked.

"North of the derelict. Underground. She's not ready yet. You can ride with me or Ceil and Auri. The moon will be set by the time we get home. I'll make tea and we can greet the sunrise."

He chose to ride with the androids.

…

Auri and the others came in and Ceil immediately began unloading the sled. Auri went up to his post, leaving Zack to join me. At table for food and water.

He wanted to know more about the Carrion Worm.

"Where are they from?" He asked, taking a sip, careful not to spill any in his mask.

"Of late, it would be the planet Eon VI, the En'Duri home world. They are used to clean up large battlegrounds. The more dead, the quicker they breed to clean up. Once done, they turn on each other until only one is left, or they all go to ground to sleep, digesting their food until the next battle."

"Similar creatures are used in the trash holds on large ships to devour discarded food and bodies." Ceil said. "Though they are not so large and offensive."

"They could lay dormant for ages," I said.

"Auri says to inform you that it is almost dawn, Captain Mag'rel."

"Thank Auri for me", I rose from the table, "Join me?"

The stars above were paling, as was the sky. Stepping out further from the ship, I began my morning song

Darkness flees, the stars lose their luster,

Bowing down to a brighter light, the new day.

I greet thy warmth, a new beginning dawns

For myself and those about on this world so blessed.

Come, Dawnbringer, I await your blessed arrival.


The first bright light of day hit the ground before me and She was there, to the shock of all but Ceil and myself.

I went to my knee before the dark haired, pale skinned woman in gold, red and yellow armor. She took my head in her hands, bowing down to kiss my forehead.

Then she stood, looking around at Zack, who seemed more than a little shocked.

"Good morning Zack Harrisson," she said. "I am Dawnbringer. My stay will be short."

"Do I know you?" Zack asked, looking confused.

"Look north. What do you see?"

North was the wreck of a scout ship, holed in a way similar to the Saurian ships and the cruise ships.

"My ship." He took a single step toward it, then looked back at Dawnbringer, confused.

"Your tale will help solve a mystery and, perhaps bring justice to this plane. When I go, you will remember and Horustondis will draw it out. Then you will be free of this place." She looked at me. "Free to deliver your message to those who will hear and listen."

"Thank you, Dawnbringer," I said.

And she was gone.

Back inside the derelict, I had my book and writing kit on the wrought iron table, ready for Zack's story. Ceil sat with us, curious about what was to happen.

"Scout Harrisson will speak and you will draw what he saw?" Ceil asked.

"The first time I did it was in a place where magic was guaranteed not to work. I drew and made a lot of money that night and on many nights there after."

"How?" Ceil asked. "If not magic-what?"

"No clue," I said, dipping the quill in the inkpot. Scout Harrisson, when you are ready…"

Four pages laid side by side showing a chaotic scene that was horrifying.

A cruise ship being torn apart by men, women and children: Saurian freighters taking on salvage and passengers bound in chains, bodies being dumped down an embankment. Overseeing it all were men in black uniforms, from dark, heavily armed and armored ships.

I'd stopped drawing and pulled the pages out, looking at what Zack had witnessed. It wasn't at all pleasant.

"I went to the nearest planet with an office of the cruise line and told them what I'd seen. They had me lead them to the planet; I don't remember arriving." He looked at me. "What happened?"

I placed the pages back into the book, locked it and returned it to the haversack.

"You witnessed a crime and were punished for it. Only Dawnbringer saved you so justice can be served -- or, at least have a chance of being served. Do you know who the men in black were?"

"Consortium," Zack said.

"The Consortium is a group of mining corporations which work to take control of all independent mining concerns. They are believed to have been responsible for the destruction of several independent mining companies and coops, as well as...." Ceil stopped, looking right at me.

"It explains why I'm here in this body." I rose from my chair. "We have a witness. We have evidence. We have to speak to the Saurian Clan/House and let them know what happened to their leader."

"There's someone else we have to contact." Zack said. "Someone that has it in for the Consortium as bad as they have it in for him."

"Who would that be?" I asked.

"Justin Stiles and the crew of Scarlet Tempest. They've been a thorn in the Consortium's side for over ten years now, helping the independents whenever they can."

"Allies are always good to have," I said. "Now, let's go find our ship"

As I finished, the ground began to shake, we all held onto something stable.

"Auri says the epicenter is just outside," Ceil said. "The ground is rising."

"Our ship is surfacing," I said. "As soon as the tremors stop, we begin loading the ship and we are out of here."

Outside of the derelict, in the depression to the north, sat our ship, the last of the ashen soil sliding off the smooth, rounded surface of a flying saucer.

"Welcome back, my girl. I missed you."

+Companion. We will adventure again?+

"We have work to do, as always."

+Good. I want to run.+

I chuckled. "You always did."

Auri's grav sled had been loaded with the trunks and spare parts which we believed we would need on our trip. The inside of the ship was quite spacious. Ivy was able to direct us to the storage areas by lights that lined the baseboards of the walls.

Once everything was secured, the doors sealed and we found our way to the bridge.

It was, of course, a circular room. The command chair was also the pilot seat. Navigation, communication and ships operation control stations were set one step down. Before all was a viewing screen.

"Ceil, do we know where to find a Saurian Clan Lord?" I asked from the command chair.

"In orbit of the planet Oxford is Hextel, the second moon. It has a spaceport and station where many races do business," Ceil replied.

"Lay in a course for Oxford." I commanded.

"Course set, Captain Mag'rel" Ceil informed me.

"Prepare for lift off." I said. "Ivy, take us up nice and easy."

You couldn't hear the engines so much as feel them, Lift off was a near gentle push up, giving us a near gentle push down until we left the planet's gravity and were in space.

Ivy turned herself in the direction programmed and we left the system fast.

For a few moments we were holding on for dear life. Then, all sense of motion seemed to stop.

"Ceil, how long until we get to Oxford?" I asked.

"Twenty-four time units," Ceil replied.

I sat back in the chair and closed my eyes, reaching out to Ivy.

+How does it feel?

+Like running without effort, Like the wind.+

+Be careful of debris. We don't want to get holed.+

+There are sensors for that. See, hear, feel, taste, smell+

+Space has a smell?+

+Bitter cold and star metal.+ Ivy telegraphed the feelings...

Like skiing down a mountain and riding down the steepest roller-coaster at the same time.

I opened my eyes, gasping.

"Captain?" Ceil asked.

"Adrenalin rush." I said, catching my breath. "Zack, I think we should get some sleep. Be rested for our meeting with the Saurian."

"Who will pilot the ship?" Zack asked, rising from his chair.

"Ivy has it all under control," I assured him.

...

Ivy had slowed to approach the planet, Oxford, its two moons and two orbiting space stations.

The station that had the obit nearest the second moon, Hextel, was a dry dock for ships in storage.

"Captain Mag'rel," Ceil spoke. "The ship Crimson Storm is docked on that station."

"Crimson Storm?" I asked."

"The sister ship to Scarlet Tempest," Zack said. "The first ship of Justin Stiles."

 Crimson Storm had the aura of long, hard use.

One ship against many.

An ant against a dam.

According to the old saying, the ant wins.

I'd delivered a message once to a man fated to die. He took my words to heart. He died, taking his assassins and my heart, with him. He had been a captain in the Kingsguard, a protector of a prince who was learning to be a bard. His older twin was to be king.

I took the Kingsguard's Oath as he lay dying and brought the prince home when he was needed.

A Bard King is a good thing.

...

The Hextel Moon Base was a major trade spot for all space faring species.

We were lucky to get a landing bay.

Ceil, Zack and I checked in and got the list of dos, don'ts, the map of the trade locations, hotels and drinking establishments. Then we went in search of Casa What's It.

J had  chosen to wear my veiled robe, boots, gloves and hat, using a walking stick, I walked behind Ceil.

Zack walked a few paces behind, dressed like most of the humans about in worn boots, pants, shirt and jacket, toting a sidearm and a few knives.

I missed my arsenal.

Many races were represented here as workers and visitors. Every so often, I caught sight of a Consortium uniform

Lovely.

Casa Whats' It was located  on a lower, darker level of the base where quiet deals could be made in supposed privacy.

If we were blocked, there would be nothing we could do about it.

It was a crowded establishment. Even the barstools were all taken. A band was playing loud and slightly discordant.

I stood to the side of the door, letting my eyes adjust and looking over the place. Ceil had gone in to get us an audience with the current Saurian Lord. Zack stood beside me, looking about.

It was a multi-level establishment, each level and section set up for specific pleasures: gambling, dancing, listening to music, eating, drinking, and watching the caged ones dance. Scattered about the room were cages where money exchanged  hands for gambling and other paid for pleasures.

A noisy place. A busy place. A place one could hide in plain sight.

Seated at a table, alone, was an En'Duri Tom and he was looking right at me, mouth slightly open, testing the air.

That he was wearing piece armor and heavily armed was not unusual for a place like this.

"The one we need to speak with is waiting," Ceil informed us, having returned from one of the cages. We followed the android to the divided staircase that went both up and down.

We went up.

There were no guards at the door. Ceil knocked in code and a voice beyond bid us enter.

The sealed door had blocked the scent of incense, an aroma I was familiar with -Rainforest. The door closed solid behind us.

The light was low. Sitting behind an ancient, carved wood desk was a Saurian male of about middle years, unarmored, in a robe that sported a pair of familiar symbols embroidered on the front.

Ceil stood in front of the desk. I stood two steps to her right. Zack, two steps to the left.

He looked from Ceil to me, to Zack and back to me.

"Deception?" He asked.

I took off my hat and removed the veil and hood.

"Caution, your lordship." I bowed to him, hand flat against my chest in the way of the people of my home world, Eon. "An endangered species must be cautious."

"Does He know this, I wonder?" The Saurian asked, picking up a feathered fan and slowly waving it. 'What do you want?"

"It's not what I want." I snapped my fingers and held my hand out to Ceil, who handed me a small cloth bag that had been hidden in one of her compartments.

"I was recently on the planet J18-23, a dumping ground for old ships and refuse. While we were there, I chanced to find this...."

I tipped the chain and medallion from the bag and placed it on the desk before the saurian.

He set the fan down and almost reverently, picked up the piece, looking it over, a hint of mixed emotion in his eyes.

"How did you come by this?" he asked, wrapping the chain about his hand to hold the medallion on his palm.

"There were seventeen Saurian freighters, holed, stripped and nose down in an odd circular configuration. Not far away, a field of bodies. That is where I found it," I said. "Left to the land, to rot beneath the hot sun. Left to feed the Carrion Worm."

"Seventeen Saurian freighters? No survivors?"

"I was there a week and saw no one but Ceil and Auri, both androids, dumped off with the trash." I pulled a second bauble from the pouch, my destroyed slave medallion, and set it on the desk. "Cast out with the trash, freed by Ceil."

"And your other companion?" The saurian looked at Zack.

"I was there by pure chance, Your Lordship," Zack said.

"You knew the holder of that medallion? What type of trade did He and his crew do?"

"Secure transport of cargo. Each contract varied." He looked at me, eyes narrowed, "Why?"

"There were other ships on the planet with similar damage, all stripped of the inner workings, engines and equipment that could be resold. Two of the ships were cruise liners."

"My brother was no slaver." He hit the desk hard with his medallion wrapped hand.

"I never said he was. You said he'd take jobs to transport. He may not have known, at the time. The damage to the Saurian ships and the cruise liners, the way they were gutted, all the same."

"How could you tell?" he asked.

"Your pardon, Sire, Auri and I examined the damage to the vessels. It was within certain perimeters for a specific type of weaponry. We

have had visual confirmation of at least one of the vessels responsible."
Ceil looked at me. I nodded.

"We are certain that the Consortium is involved."

"Aren't they responsible for the loss of your home world? The enslavement of your people?"

This was not going well.

"We are not the only ones suffering at the hands of the Consortium," I said. "Independent miners, My home world. The people from the cruise liners are now slaves on other worlds that allow it or in the mines of the Consortium and who's to know?"

"Sire? Forgive me, but, would your brother answer a call for help?" Ceil asked. "A vast ship in trouble. Certain of monetary rewards? Auri had been on a cruise liner. His observations led him to believe that certain members of the crew were involved."

He thought for a moment. "The proof is on the planet?"

Zack brought the four pages I had drawn from his pocket and lay them before the Saurian Lord for inspection.

"I saw it all," Zack said. "Told the Cruise line office. They followed me there and shot me down. I was lucky to survive."

I replaced my hood, veil and hat, then took up the ruins of my slave medallion.

"You know what we know. Do with it what you will."

We went to the door. At first, it wouldn't open. I looked back at the Saurian Lord.

After a moment, he reached under the desk and the door opened.

The three of us left the room.

...

"That went well." I said sarcastically as we walked down the hallway.

"You told him what we knew. Showed him the truth. What he does with the information is up to him." Ceil said.

"You have a fan." Zack said as we descended the stairs.

The Tom was watching me closely.

"Ceil, Zack, wait by the door for me." I made my way to the Tom's table.

"Yes, Captain." Ceil acknowledged and they obeyed.

I sat down without asking and waited.

"Where have you been?" he asked, voice slightly trembling.

"Where was I?" I asked. He knew 'Her'. For better or worse, it was.

"Our new colony. I went for supplies. When I got back--nothing. You and the others were gone."

"How long ago was that?" I asked. This was going to be difficult.

"Four years ago," he said, close to accusation.

We should be doing this in private.

I rose from the chair.

"Come with me," I said, moving toward the exit where Ceil and Zack were waiting.

I was almost there when several men in Consortium Black walked in.

What the hell were they doing in a low end bar?

I stepped aside to let them pass, keeping my distance as most non-human species did when confronted with the near-hairless ones.

If you step aside, the arrogant ones believe it's because you are acknowledging their superiority.

The paranoid ones believe you're about to stab them in the back.

The Consortium men moved on toward the gambling tables, passing by the Tom who had put on his helmet before leaving the table, taking a route that would totally bypass the humans.

Ceil and Zack followed us out the door.

Ceil led the way back to the spaceport and Ivy.

It seemed the closer we got to the port, the more Consortium men we saw.

"Auri and Ivy ready to go?" I asked.

"Oh, yes," Ceil said.

The space port was very busy at this time of day, ships were waiting to come in, while most of the ones docked were reluctant to lift off.

The four of us entered the ship and the door shut.

"Ceil, I want you to request lift off clearance so that the ships waiting to land can hear it."

"At once, Captain Mag'rel." Ceil moved off swiftly toward the bridge with Zack right behind her.

I turned to the Tom, removing my hat and veiled hood.

"We will talk after liftoff," I promised. "You can sit in the navigators seat."

"What about your navigator?" He asked, removing his helmet as he followed me forward.

"Don't really need one, actually." The gloves came off and went into the hat. "I'll explain everything once we're safely out of here."

Ceil was receiving clearance when we arrived on the bridge.

Sitting in the command chair, I dropped my hat and gloves on the floor before the chair and put my feet on them.

"Take a seat and prepare for liftoff." He obeyed at once, being careful not to touch anything.

"Ivy, take us out of here," I said.

There was a brief vibration and the ship rose, slowly at first. When the bottom of the vessel had cleared the bay, the ship accelerated up.

"Captain, what is our destination?" Ceil asked.

"I want to see home," I said. He looked back at me, stunned: "I need a place to start."

He turned back to the board and put in the destination.

The ship stopped, turned in the targeted direction and...

"Hold on," I said, as Ivy took off at full speed ahead.

Once again, at speed, it didn't feel as if we were moving at all.

Picking up my hat and gloves, I left my seat, stepping up behind the Tom.

"Let's go get reacquainted, you and I?"

…

We raided the icebox and sat at the short end of a long table.

"Four years," I said. "You've been searching for four years." Statement, not question. "I've known a few with that kind of devotion." I continued before he could speak. "Is her name Mag'rel?"

"Yes," he said. "I am Mou'ant. How can you not know me?"

"I don't remember anything until Ceil took the slave amulet from my neck," I said, toying with my food. "I know I am En'duri. I know where We come from, Pride, Pack and Tribe. I know history, the distant past. I just don't know us."

"What did they do to you?" He asked.

"Some slaves are treated badly," I said. "Perhaps they treated this one so cruelly that all memory of the torture and pain drove everything out?"

I sensed the sadness, saw the bright, yellow eyes filling with tears.

"I came back as soon as I could…"

I pushed the plate away. "She was pregnant?" He nodded, but looked puzzled.

I got up and started pacing.

She had told me. Dawnbringer had said that the loss of her kids had broken her.

I sat down, hard. I had to speak the truth.

"Mou'ant, what I have to say will sound crazy, but it is the truth." I looked at him. "Ready?"

He nodded.

"My name is Horustondis Magpie. My patron, Dawnbringer, has sent me here on a mission. Mag'rel's spirit is currently in my true body. I've been told she is recovering from the trauma that the slavers put her through and that when I have completed my mission, she will be returned to this body. Dawnbringer says she should be alright by then."

He wants to believe, fantastic as the story is.

"Remember your history?" I asked. "The stories of the Bard King? The first trade agreements with the Kal Zestri? The Qui La Rue? The-

"-War with the Daemeous." He nodded.

"The tall human female with the orange red hair who drew pictures and took a Kingsguards' Oath?"

"Tales the ancients used to tell," he nodded, then asked, "Was it true? About the half breed kit who was made whole?"

"Yes. Dawnbringer and three very powerful Qui La Rue made her whole." I said. Reaching out, I took his hand.

"Dawnbringer will return your mate to you when this is over."

"Your word?" He asked.

"I cannot lie. She gave her word and I've never known her to go back on it."

He thought about it for a long time.

"I will stay with you until then."

# Technicolor

## By Shannan Volters

Shannan Volters currently resides in Cincinnati, OH where she spends her free time rock climbing, reading, and generally geeking out. She has been a lifelong book lover and writer, with her first story being three sentences about a bear in the woods. She currently blogs about books and the writing life at shannanwithana.com

~~~

"On your feet Violet." The guard flipped his baton causing it to triple in length. "Don't try anything. Blossom is coming with us."

"Frank, do you really think I would try to run from you?" I hoped the sweetness didn't cover my sarcasm. "You're my favorite Brown after all." My tongue numbed at the lie. Even though Blossom made it possible for me to say anything I wanted, true or not, there was still a discomfort to it I could never get used to.

"You say that to all of us." Frank's mouth and eyes were matching slits, as he examined every word I said. He was always scared by the possibility I could know every last thing about him.

"Don't you want to know the truth?" I sauntered close with my cuffed hands before me, daring him to unlock them. "We can leave Blossom here and have some fun."

Frank put the end of his baton on my chest, preventing me from coming closer.

"Lily wants to see you."

"Lily White?"

"What other Lily would I be talking about?"

I groaned. This could only mean trouble-- for everyone.

"Why do you work for her?" I asked. Frank let his baton fall as I took the lead on the familiar path to the office.

"It's good money." Frank said, following close behind. "You know what that's like."

"And look where it got me," I said as I whipped around to face him, causing Frank to stumble to a stop just before impact, "you should pray you wind up this well off."

It wasn't Truth. It was a truth, but not my Violet Truth. Not the kind that cuts through the façade of life to the hidden reality of the heart. Frank knew that. But that didn't stop him from checking every two steps that Blossom was still following behind us. Sweat from beading on his forehead.

It took ten minutes to make it to Lily's office. It took another ten for me to convince myself to walk through the door. Lily was a collector: people, debts, secrets, anything that would ensure she kept her place of power. And if she was calling me to her office, it meant she had her eye on a new collectible.

"I have a job for you." Lily didn't look up from the papers she was reading.

"I know." I blinked a couple times stepping into the "Void of Color" as I liked to call it. Really, it was "the Void of All But One Color," but that was a long name for the small room, and "The White Room" was boring.

"I need a truth revealed," Lily said.

"Does that mean I'm losing my Orange." I glanced behind me, knowing the door blocked Blossom from view.

"Once you're outside these walls."

"I want to stay outside these walls."

"No."

"Then no." I crossed my arms.

Finally, she looked at the wall behind me, which was the closest anyone had ever come to looking me in the eyes. Most people think if you look a Color in the eyes, no matter what, they can use their Ability on you. I didn't believe it, but no one was ever daring enough to see how true it was.

"If I let you stay outside, you must still come when I need you," Lily told me. This had to be a big Truth for her to be letting me outside alone. It had to be even bigger for her to agree to let me stay.

All I could do is nod. So close to freedom I couldn't even breathe. The chance to be Violet again, to be me again.

"I'll send Turk after you if you don't."

I swallowed hard. The only time I'd ever seen Turk was when he brought me in. I didn't trust anyone that didn't have any Truths to reveal. Granted, I didn't typically trust anyone with Truths either.

"Understood?" Lily raised an eyebrow; at least I think that's what she was trying to do since she has no hair.

"Fine." I resumed my hardened disdain as Lily unlocked the top drawer of her desk and pulled out a single book. Thin and pocket size, she placed it on the desk and pushed it to the edge.

"You have five days," is all she said, then pressed a nearly invisible white button.

"Frank, if you will come in." Frank entered and took the book and then handed it to me.

"You'll find the Truth you're looking for in that book." I flipped through the pages then read the cover. A black and white book called "Peter Pan" I had never heard of.

"Do I get help?"

"You don't need help."

I would have objected, but, with the number of Blues in the museum, I'm sure she worked out the best possible future. I turned and walked out of the office straight to the side exit. Frank followed with Blossom at his side.

"How long?" Frank asked, removing the handcuffs and handing over my bag.

"Hopefully forever." It was only his eyes that showed surprise, widening ever so slightly. If I hadn't been looking for it, I would have missed it.

"Make sure you wear your weapon." It almost sounded like he was concerned for me, but then I knew better. He was protecting Lily's asset.

"See you around Orange Blossom." Blossom's scowl made me grin. She hated any reference to her color. It's why she wore brown colored contacts. And, since she only had one marker, most people never knew she was Orange. Not like me. I had all three markers: eyes, hair, and skin: a Violet through and through, and I loved it. I couldn't understand Blossom, or anyone for that matter, who didn't want their color.

I heard the door click behind me and knew Frank and Blossom had left as I felt my Ability strengthening; it was a muscle that had atrophied from five years in the museum, and I needed to stretch it out.

But it would have to wait. I had to find Emmy.

It was the first time a car wasn't waiting for me, further proof I was flying under the radar. But, after a couple rights and lefts, I found a familiar street crossing and started toward Molly's Bar.

No one knew anymore why it was called that. The owner, Ice, came from a long line of Technicolors. He tried to convince us from time to time that his great-great-whatever coined the phrase in reference to the old TV's when they switched from black and white to color sets.

"Looks like us humans are finally catching up." He would say in a mocking voice passed down through their family.

The bell jingled as I walked in the door.

"I don't know where Emmy is Blues to see into the future was something I could never get completely used too.

" Why don't you know?" I said with a hard edge, a warning to those that know me I was going to find the truth, one way or another.

"B...b...before you go all V...v....violet on me, I'll t...tell you." He looked just over my right shoulder as he stuttered out his response, the only sign of fear. That was the worst part about being violet. Even the people closest to you were still afraid of what you would find out about them, and what you would do as a result. "She left three years ago and hasn't been back."

"Three years?" I didn't need to study Ice further to know he was telling the truth. "Do you know where she went?"

"Away" is all she said. She knew Turk would be sent after her, and she didn't want to leave a trail." Ice laid his pale blue hand on my deep purple one. "Sorry Violet."

"Sorry?" I was trying to control my breathing, but it wasn't working. And the drumming of blood in my ears didn't help. "You said you'd watch after her. She was twelve years old, and you just let her leave?"

"You said you needed me to watch her for the night, which turned into two years," Ice said, as he flung my hand away. He was prepared for this moment, knowing I would come back one day.

"I should go." It was an inaudible mumbling that didn't need repeating. Ice already knew, and I needed air. Emmy was gone, and, without a Green as good as Emmy, there was no way I would have a chance of finding her, which meant I never would.

The ally behind the bar didn't do anything but provide a place to breakdown. Emmy, my baby girl and I let her down. I was supposed to protect her. I should have fought harder to escape the museum. Now who knows where she is or if I'll ever see her again.

I let my head fall as I hugged my knees to my chest. The heat of my sobs quickly made it difficult to breath, but I refused to look up. The only chance left was to succeed at this mission. I had to be free so I could find Emmy.

Once the tears stopped spilling down my face, I blindly groped for the book Lily had given me. My hand grazed cool metal before finding the novel, and I contemplated leaving the gun there. But being alone without open communication made it seem wise to at least have the appearance of protection. No one had to know I would never use it.

After securing the weapon to my hip, I opened "Peter Pan" to page 8, the number of missions I had been on. At first, there was only a slight shimmer to the pages, letting me know there was more to the book than a story. Soon, my mind was rearranging phrases and words until all that remained was a picture, a name, and a single sentence. And if I wasn't a Violet, I wouldn't have believed it.

There was a new Ability.

Generations ago, the first Ability presented. CustomKids© had been a company that gave over-zealous parents the chance to pick out everything they wanted in a child, from looks to personality to talents. For the right price, you could have the perfect kid.

But then those kids grew up and had kids, and that's what accelerated human DNA: Two CustomKids© falling in love and having natural kids. Within 10 years, there was a whole rainbow of children in schools and daycares around the world.

It wasn't until that first child hit puberty that panic started to hit. Every news station in the world covered it for weeks: the Yellow child could make plants grow. It wasn't much longer before they realized every Technicolor kid had some kind of Ability.

So, as humans have done time and time again, they put all the Unknowns in a cage and waited to see what would happen. A whole generation lived in a bubble with only each other as company, which meant they also fell in love with each other, making their abilities stronger. These were the colors that broke out and forced their way into the world. They made them, and now they would have to live with them.

A new color, though, seemed impossible. There were a finite amount of colors, and, we learned long ago, hues didn't matter. Red and pink were the same, just as emerald and lime were the same. The only thing that affected our abilities was how many markers you had: one, two, or three. But, by now, my Ability had returned to full strength, making the truth plain as day: there was a new color, and a new, unknown Ability. No wonder Lily sent me and gave me my freedom. It was worth the risk of losing me if there was a chance of being the first and only collector with a new color in their museum, even if it wound up being as lame as an Orange.

I closed my eyes, leaning my head back against the brick wall, and let the fall air dry my face. I would have been content to stay there the next five days till Lily sent Turk after me, when the bell to the bar jingled. A boy with red hair and a shimmer over one eye was standing at the door. He wasn't moving, which made me think he was in a virtual communication room. Really bad timing if that's the case because the next person to leave the bar was going to knock him across the street. The thought made me smile. Until I realized who he was.

I reached for my bag, the quick acting adrenaline causing my fingers to fumble at the ties.

"There is no way it could be this easy." I said, opening the book back up and scrambling for the page with the picture on it. I had no sooner reformed the picture to compare him, than he turned and walked away.

"You've got to be kidding me." I muttered throwing my bag on my back, prepared to chase after the boy with a Secret. I rounded the corner after him, and there he stood in the middle of the street, waiting for me.

"Hello Violet." The boy stood with his hands clasped in front of him and a tell tale shimmer over his right eye. "Name's Dominic Rose."

So I was right. This was the boy I was looking for. I reached in my bag, fishing for the communicator. Lily wouldn't expect this quick of a response.

"I'll take that." I had been so focused on Dominic that I hadn't seen the four other people come behind me, blocking my escape. I really was rusty.

"Who are they?", I asked the boy.

"They are also Dominic Rose." He paused "Actually, maybe it's more accurate to say we are all a Dominic Rose. He straightened his prism checkered bow tie, as though nothing was out of the ordinary."What really matters is why I'm here."

"And why are you here?" I crossed my arms, annoyed he was telling the truth. But it was obvious his eye was hiding something, so I tried to focus any spare attention I had to unraveling that mystery.

"I'm here about the next stage of genetics."

"What do you mean?" I hoped he took my stare as annoyed anger rather than an attempt to discover his Truth.

"Dominic Rose is a code phrase we use to identify second stage abilities." Dominic fiddled with his shirt sleeves, tugging them ever so slightly so they would show under the cuff of his jacket. "Hue matters now."

"Wait. What?" I couldn't make my mind compute what he was saying.

"We are no longer confined to the basic 8 colors. The possibilities are now endless, and with this next stage of development two possible futures exist. And you are the only one who can decide which future happens."

"Me? Why me?"

"Because that's the way it worked out. Eon here," Dominic motioned to the second person on the left who slightly nodded his head, "has the Ability not only to see into the future, but see how decisions and actions affect the future. And he has taken every path possible with only two possibilities existing, both revolving around your choice."

His words were grating on my ears. He was lying about something. "How could something I do make that big a difference on the world?" I asked.

"It is rarely the well known people that make a difference but the people that brave the monotony of an average life who bring about great change. Sometimes it can never be traced to them, but still their everyday choices can lead to a better world. Today is your day of choice."

"So what are my choices then?" The skepticism in my voice was clear, and Dominic seemed to have sympathy apparent by the disbelief written on his face.

"Maybe if I explain the future first." Dominic reached for his bag, pulled a small metal ball from it, and tossed it in the air where it floated above his head. He made a few motions with his hands and brought up a world map in the space between us with dots of the colors on it. While Brown was still a large portion, Orange, Red, and Yellow were starting to grow. The other colors were still an obvious minority.

"As you can see, Techni's are still working their way into a present minority, let alone majority. At the current rate we've been moving, it will still be another century before we can tell a large difference in the map. But here is where the future separates. One of your choices will not only push us into the majority, but also allow our powers to start crossing over."

"What does that mean? That Browns will have powers too?"

"No", Dominic said as he put a finger to his right eye, "It means this." And when his contact came out, the shimmer dissipated, and I understood why I couldn't see past the haze: I didn't know it was even a possibility, let alone reality.

"You have two different colored eyes." It seemed so matter of fact when it came out of my mouth, but my heart was racing in panic. That wasn't possible.

"Yes. And a new and unique power to show for it." I continued to stare above his red and yellow eyes that gave him a sickly look.

"So what's your new Ability?"

"DNA manipulation. I can tell living cells what to do."

"So can you manipulate people?"

"No. Not exactly. I can make their body listen to me, even if their mind is contradicting everything I say."

"So you can make me walk off a bridge or something?"

"Or something." Was all Dominic said in a disinterested way.

"So what's the other option?" I said, trying not to look at his eyes.

70

"The other future is where Technis don't exist at all."

I stared at him in disbelief for a while. "How is that even possible? We're here, and it's not like they are trying to string us up a tree or burn us at the stake or something."

"They put us in museums. And since we're comfortable and well fed, we get lazy and stop trying to make a better life for ourselves. Eventually we all die off and the world goes back to the way things were, and we become a story parents tell their kids at bedtime."

I stared at Dominic for a while. Not sure whether I want to believe him or not. There was no shimmer or haze to point out any lies; no goosebumps or chills to make me disbelieve his words.

"So." I braced myself for the worst. "Do you know what I'm going to pick?"

"It doesn't work like that." Eon's voice was deep and husky. "I know what will happen no matter what you choose, but it's still up to you."

" And now that you know what futures you're picking between, you have one choice." Dominic seemed put out that Eon said anything. "Either you do this, or you don't. But it has to be your choice. Techni's end up dead in the futures where we force this on you, or kill you, or we would have done it already."

"Well that's comforting."

Dominic paused, letting the past few moments sink in before he spoke again. "You will need to give up your power."

I stared at Dominic, not sure I heard him right.

"You want me to do what?"

"You need to let Ebony take away your abilities." Dominic waved his hand at the Girl that had silently moved next to me. She had black eyes and hair, but otherwise pale skinned. It was an eerie sight to see.

"But," I opened and closed my mouth a couple times, not sure what to say. "How?" Is all I could come up with.

"She can remove powers permanently." His words caused no ringing in my ears, but I still examined Dominic's face, looking for anything to show he was lying.

"I can't." Saying it out loud I knew made it true. It was Truth. How could I give up the one thing that made me, me. I was Violet, through and through.

I tried swallowing the lump in my throat. It was too much to ask. I felt myself plop onto the ground, the weight of what was being asked hitting me. It would be so simple to give up everything, to be normal with no reason for anyone to chase me or the ability to chase anyone else. But who would I be if I wasn't a violet?

"Why me?" I asked, uncertain of this role I had been thrust into.

"Because of Emmy."

My head jolted up, and I almost looked Dominic in the eyes. "What do you know about Emmy?"

"I know in five years Lily finally collects her, which means she permanently collects you. You would do anything to keep Emmy safe, even if it meant the destruction of all of us."

"That can't be true." But the whisper never left my mouth. I know it's Truth from my inability to contradict it. "And what happens to Emmy if I give up my powers?"

"Let's just say, she'll be safe." His smile widened as my eyes did. "Come now. You didn't think it was a happy accident that our paths crossed, did you? We used the best tracker around. And I'm sure you know who I'm talking about."

"I want to see her."

"Plenty of time for that. But first you need to make a choice."

"Or what? You'll kill..." But I couldn't finish the sentence. It was either the emotions of the thought, or the fact it wasn't Truth. But in the moment, it didn't matter.

"Of course not. We'll just make sure, if you decide to continue life with your powers, that you never see Emmy again. It will be a more difficult future for us, but at least it will be a future."

"So you're making me give up my abilities."

"No. You still get to choose. You can keep your abilities and we'll let you walk out of here safe and sound, just like we told you. But we also couldn't risk your keeping your powers and Lily finding Emmy."

"And if I give up my abilities, what happens to Emmy then?"

"Whatever the two of you decide."

My ears felt like they were vibrating for the volume of lies and half truths. Dominic was incapable of being honest. "I want to talk to Emmy."

Dominic sighed. "I was afraid it would come to that." He waved his hand flippantly, and the orb spun, throwing a static image onto an ally wall.

"Emmy?" I called out.

"Mom? Is that you?" The image was unclear, but the voice was obviously Emmy's. For the second time in a day, tears were poring down my face.

"Emerald." The whisper was enough for her to hear and scrunch her face.

"You know I hate you using my full name."

"I know."

"Are you coming to see me?" I could hear the strain in her voice. Something wasn't right. "I miss you."

"I'll see you soon Emmy."

As I said goodbye to Emmy, I knew there was another choice. One they either ignored or believed impossible. But in that moment, I knew it was the only option. It would also require more sacrifice than just loosing my color. It would require me to loose myself as well.

"Is there no other choice?" I said more to myself as I felt the Violet slipping away, uncertain who would replace her.

"This is the only choice." Dominic said as he looked straight into my eyes, trying to force me to make my decision.

I looked back into his eyes as I pulled out the gun and asked for one last truth. "What would you do?"

Then I pulled the trigger.

.

# Star Date

## By Stacy Bender

Stacy Bender lives in Cincinnati with her cat, Montgomery Python (she loves bad puns), and her husband-- fellow science fiction/fantasy writer, Reid Minnich.

She has always had a wild imagination and dreamed of writing a book ever since she saw the movie 'The Ghost and Mrs. Muir' when she was young. Stacy has the unusual habit of writing her stories in her head before ever attempting to put them on paper.

Her eclectic interests vary from gardening, antiques, reading, writing, cooking, and spending time with good friends.

~~~

Star date 3-3-152. The aliens still remain my captives, but I wonder for how long. The male seems resistant to my psionic training, unlike the female who responds quite nicely. Subtle commands are all that are necessary now.

One of them tried hiding my holographic refractor shield the other day while I was resting. It was an abysmal attempt, but then neither of the creatures show much in the way of intelligence. Removal from its hiding place was easily obtained. Once the shield is activated, navigating the creatures' enclosure requires some effort as their habitat requires multiple cushiony structures to support their rather rigid and bony frames. But I can accomplish this with a practiced ease.

The male doesn't notice me as I pass. It never does. But the female seems to have extra sensory powers. She glances in my direction before resuming whatever it is that she's doing. I must get a closer look. The noises that I hear are tantalizingly sweet, and the smell is hauntingly appealing.

Oh no, it can't be. The female has the insidious long range aether super energy redactafior. How is it possible? I destroyed it the other day. Its power is unstoppable.

I must resist, or my name isn't James T. K.......

"Why do you think he does that?" he asked.

"Does what?"

"Chase the red dot. The only reason he came out from under the couch was because you bought him a new laser pointer."

"He loves it. Don't you Captain Kitty?"

# Phoenix Seven

## By Timothy Attewell

 Timothy Attewell has a passion for all forms of storytelling. He has spent years working in the film and television industry while writing and directing short films of his own. However, not all stories are meant for the screen. Attewell's writing aims to express and explore ideas that are simply too internal, complex or oddball for the audio-visual medium. Attewell enjoys reading and writing a wide range of genres including Sci-Fi, Horror, Mystery/Detective, Comedy and Political Satire. His recent Novella, "Marathon," incorporates a delicate combination of all of these genres. For inspiration, Tim looks to Jonathan Lethem, Chuck Palahniuk, Stephen King, H.P. Lovecraft, Nicholson Baker, Richard Matheson and Phillip K. Dick.

~~~

P lease don't let anyone else read this.

I do understand how you might feel about such a request. You don't really know me. For that matter, you owe me positively nothing.

Still, I must beg you to extend to me this singular kindness and keep these words to yourself.

I should tell you who I am; a geologist, for starters. My name is Dr. Wade Edwards. I know as much as anyone can about what this planet is made of. Due to the nature of this message I suppose I should also specify that the planet I'm referring to is Earth.

If we ever do meet, you may call me Wade. Please spare me the "Doctor" prefix as such a term is reserved for colleagues and I would like to consider us friends.

Before I ask for your help, let me explain how my associates and I have found ourselves in this situation.

These events were set in motion when a man I have never met chose a new location for his target shooting. Having already had his wrists slapped once for discharging weapons too close to a peaceful residential area, he opted to move his activities a few kilometers further outside his small desert town.

Within those rocky hills, he was free to target shoot all the live-long day. I suppose it must have taken him a while, but eventually he noticed a discrepancy that perturbed his detail-oriented mind.

Any time he returned home from this place, he observed that his wristwatch had fallen out of sync with the rest of the world. It was rarely by much, but also never consistent. Two minutes ahead, three minutes behind, etc.

His first conclusion was that the recoil of his twelve-gauge was causing damage to the inner workings of his watch. So he stopped wearing it all together.

The next oddity that occurred was harder for the man to explain. When out with friends one evening as the sun was setting, the local radio station he had been playing went dead.

The static halted all conversation and gunfire, as it was no ordinary analog hiss. This static had a whining quality, similar to stressed metal. With everyone's attention on the sound, suddenly the radio station returned. One of the man's friends quickly noticed that the news update played at the top of the hour was for Tuesday, October 9th. It being the 5th, this raised a few eyebrows. Days later the events of the news report came true and the men began to take the occurrence seriously.

I imagine the marksman had some trouble convincing the university of these occurrences, but eventually he did. Once a few tests confirmed the existence of an anomaly, the physicists were called first. They always are.

Using radios and atomic clocks, they determined the anomaly had a radius of some six meters. I'm told that during this phase they picked up broadcasts from the 1983 general election, a Pennsylvania weather report from a particularly cold day during the World War and a Mexican sports broadcast detailing a football match that had not yet occurred.

If all of this seems too fictitious, you can feel free to visit our exact location (which I am getting to) and have a listen for yourself. I only ask that you please go alone and above all else, tell no one of what you hear.

Now, having hit a bit of a dead end, they reached out to minds of different disciplines and invited them to the site. One of these minds was mine. While astronomers looked above for cause and explanation, I looked below.

My theory was that something had impacted the site long before man. If this item had been from reaches of space we couldn't even conceive of, then it would be reasonable to suggest that it was not governed by common laws of physics.

The university was skeptical, but among the other more mystic theories, mine was the most sound. To test my theory we dug a series of three-meter deep holes. My hope was that the effects of the anomaly would intensify, but they didn't do exactly that.

The malfunctioning clock-effect quickly dropped off, and it was difficult to hear displaced radio broadcasts since the dirt blocked out most signals. What we did find, however, was that in the absence of earthly radio signals, we could hear even more clearly the intense metallic, whining moan, apparently being transmitted from below. Those of us who spent a great deal of time at the site came to nickname the sounds "Iron Whales."

Our preliminary digging taught us that we weren't simply dealing with a circular plot of land with strange properties. The deeper we dug, the wider the anomaly. It became clear that what the marksman had discovered was merely the surface tip of a very large sphere of influence.

By gauging the strength of the signal in each hole, we were able to determine the anomaly's size and thereby triangulate its center. The area of influence was massive. With a diameter of more than one-kilometer, we knew we would have to dig just over six hundred meters straight down to find the disturbance's center.

The university commenced digging at once. So far outside of town, none of us ever once thought that our discovery could bring harm to the nearby residents, let alone the world.

•••

Tunneling down to the center took nine months. Very early on in the process, we began encountering shards of a substance that was most assuredly not of this Earth.

This of course came as a great relief to me, as I had suspected I might have to wait until we reached the anomaly's center before I had any materials to analyze. Bringing the samples back to the university was a feeling more gleeful than any academic award I had ever won.

Much to my disappointment, upon investigation in the lab, the shard's effects on time and radio waves seemed to be completely nullified. Fortunately, the objects carried a variety of other exotic traits.

They were typically no larger than a man's arm and carried next to no weight at all. They were colored a vibrant lemon yellow and were smooth as glass. Tapping them with so much as the tip of my fingernail would produce a tremendous clanking sound, yet for some reason when one sample collided with another, they made no sound at all.

As digging continued we noticed a pattern in the material's distribution. The shards were pointed long-ways away from the center of the anomaly we were attempting to reach. Though there were no signs of intense heat or impact, this is what we surmised:

The samples had impacted the earth as a singular, larger object. Rather than obliterating on contact as most meteoroids do, this object remained intact as it ripped into Earth's crust. There it must have sat for eons, a unit of time I was hoping to narrow down with study, though I fear now I may never know.

For any number of reasons, (the cooling of the earth's crust or perhaps a change in pressure from seismic activity), the object exploded into countless pieces. The shards cut outward through dirt and rock, ending up in a roughly a spherical dispersal pattern.

This explained partially why the lone samples lost their most bizarre effects once separated from the group. As single samples they produced no distortion in time, but as a larger whole, distributed properly, they created a disruptive field. This made me think that after the digging was done, we would find nothing at the center of the anomaly, but again I was wrong.

The drill was supposed to ease down and back off before reaching dead center of the anomaly's sphere of influence. Though the operator claims ignorance, I suspect it was ego that drove him forward. The machine continued to function, churning away its enormous bit, and at one point, forward progress completely halted.

The machine was reversed, and what we found confirmed to all that we were knocking on a dangerous door. The front half of the massive drill bit had ceased to exist. It was not melted, ground, or cut off, but was simply no longer there. Had the operator continued down his path I imagine he along with the whole of the machine would have been gone forever.

This created a pivotal shift in the project's direction. No longer were we digging for our prize. We had found it. Now, instead, we would build a research facility around it, a particularly odd area of space we came to call "The Event."

•••

My own relevance to the project was called into question. With no more earthly or celestial matter to analyze, research had swung heavily in the direction of theoretical physics. On top of this, a rapid increase in secrecy and protocol developed around the project. I didn't realize it at the time, but in fighting for my right to remain on the project, I was battling for my very existence.

I'm sad to say that I was kept around only in part for my ability to contribute to the research going forward. Mostly, I feel I was permitted to stay as a means of being kept quiet.

This battle for involvement kept me out of the lab for the majority of its construction. Once I was finally granted access, riding the elevator car down, I was barely able to maintain my professional composure;

fidgeting and humming with excitement. As I stepped into the Lab's main room, what I beheld made me feel small. Like an insignificant speck in a universe I would never truly understand.

The lab was a massive, wide-open space the size of an airplane hangar. At its center, seemingly hovering five meters off the ground was The Event. A series of busy catwalks had been constructed around it, and an impressive array of sensors and equipment around that.

It is difficult to do justice the exact look of The Event. You could say it had no look at all. Though The Event itself was technically invisible, looking through it I could see what would have been had the site never been discovered. It was like looking through a lens that was pointed directly at the Earth's crust.

The Event was two meters in diameter, and like its larger area of influence, a perfect sphere. I stepped around it and marveled at the stomach-turning change in perspective that occurred. I wasn't seeing a sphere covered in rock, but rather, a sphere that always had rock on its opposite side, but never the one facing me.

The catwalks above were crawling with technicians, flurrying all about, tinkering with odd devices that had been mounted onto the railing. Apparently some sort of sensor, the devices were reminiscent of the lights that hang over all dentist's chairs, though instead of a blinding bulb on the end of the support arm, there was a receiving dish.

Before I had the chance to step closer, I was pulled away to my small corner of the facility. In a room separate from The Event, I was to continue my studies on the yellow shards of material that had been recovered during the excavation.

There weren't many more samples, as per my instructions diggers had done their best to leave them undisturbed. The concern was that if enough of them had been relocated, the field they created would destabilize and cease to exist entirely.

Though I had already performed nearly all the tests I could conceive of, this was an opportunity to analyze the fragments' behavior from within the field itself. Perhaps there was still something to be learned there.

Regardless, my interests laid elsewhere. I did my best to spend as much time in The Event room as possible. I took frequent bathroom breaks; at lunch I spoke with the physicists. Sometimes I would even invent nonsensical questions for technicians just to justify getting closer to that fascinating focal point of the anomaly.

Peering into The Event was unlike any sight I had ever seen. The physicists likened it to the event horizon of a black hole (the source of its name). If you were to look at any black hole, you would see a wide disk of matter and particles spiraling around an increasingly strong center of gravity. The point at which gravity is so strong, not even light could escape it is known as the event horizon. Hence, blackness.

Our Event, however, instead of being at the center of a black hole of gravity, was a black hole of time. The bubble at the center of the field was a perfect sphere from which time could not escape. When looking through The Event, I imagine the dirt and rock we were seeing was from the meteoroid's time of impact.

A geologists dream, you might say, to behold the makings of our planet as they were billions of years ago. More than anything, I felt compelled to reach out and touch what The Event was showing, but it had been established that no one or thing should be allowed to physically interact with The Event until it was fully understood; a policy thought to be wise, considering what had happened to our drill.

Having lurked long enough, it soon became clear to me. The technicians were mapping The Event. Any given point on its surface corresponded with its very own place and time on earth. The satellite dish-looking receivers could pick up radio broadcasts emanating from within The Event. A dish pointed at a given square centimeter would pick up a signal from China in 1980, one centimeter to the left would produce strange music from a year we gathered to be 2092.

I found myself wondering what would be the project's next step once the mapping phase was complete. I went on like this, clocking in and clocking out each day, doing little more than pondering what the future held. Then came the night when it all went wrong.

•••

I was sitting quietly in my lab, dreaming of what this discovery meant for mankind. My own research had reached a stalemate, and my job quickly became looking busy whenever I received a visitor. The larger implications of The Event's potential fully occupied my thoughts. Surely, with enough study we could one day find a way to send a message, or even a human being through time.

What then, would occur if we sent a man back in time to the marksman? If we steered him clear of his new target range, and the anomaly had never been discovered, would the lab then cease to exist? It was a classic paradox. I often contemplated it not so much to find a solution as much as to enjoy being a part of one.

All at once, the lights in the room died. With all power lost, my first thought was this was how they were telling me to pack my things. The notion of being laid off was rapidly trumped by the mild tremor that shook my lab. Something was wrong.

It surprised me how ill prepared I had been for a power loss. In pitch black, I fumbled to the nearest wall then followed it to the door.

The power was out in the hallway as well. Though most of the scientists had left hours ago, I could hear the remainder of the team making commotion in The Event room. Finally, the backup lights came to life and I made my way to the heart of the facility.

There were six technicians that had either stayed late or just begun their night shift. For the sake of the record, their names were: Connor Starr, Oliver Bishop, Matthew Holt, Albert Henry, Stacy Pierce, and Alice Mann.

They gathered beneath The Event, flashlights in hand. Wanting to avoid interrupting with a clueless question, I gleaned what had happened by overhearing their discussion.

While constructing a new catwalk above The Event, Connor had dropped a two-inch steel bolt. It plummeted downward and promptly disappeared into The Event. The facility lost power instantly.

I spoke up. Perhaps the bolt had been caught at the focal point of the field, generating an electromagnetic pulse that disrupted our flow of power.

Regardless of cause, to exit the facility, we certainly wouldn't be using the elevator. Climbing out was the only option. Though I felt tempted to stay below and enjoy this alone time with The Event, I felt being the one to deliver important news to the surface would only bolster my dwindling relevance to the project.

The night-shifters opted to stay. Some of their work could continue without power, at least until we reached the surface and notified the university of the hiccup.

Ascending the ladder took longer than I would have expected. Alice, Matt, Al and I made the half kilometer climb, occasionally stopping to rest our fatigued arms and legs. With each rung up, darker thoughts about what could have gone wrong crept in. We were dealing with a force of unknown power. What if the theorized electromagnetic pulse had encompassed the whole of the Earth? It was entirely possible that we had turned out the lights of the world.

Stepping out onto the surface yielded only a brief sense of relief. The sun had just set moments ago, but the sky was still bright. Enough to illuminate for all of us to see: the project's surface presence had completely disappeared. Parking lot, guard gate, supply bins, all had vanished. The only evidence of the project having ever existed was the open elevator shaft leading to the lab far beneath our feet.

A group decision was made: Al would climb back down to inform the others that they might be further from having power restored than we initially thought. Matt, Alice and I would walk to town. I disregarded it as atmospheric illusion at the time, but the lights seemed to cast an unusually bright glow into the sky that night. I would soon discover the true source of the glow.

•••

When we returned to the lab from our visit to town, the rest of the team greeted us with fearful eyes. They had been left in the dark facility, sitting beneath The Event for hours while the three of us completed our excursion.

To say I didn't know how to explain our findings to them would be a stretch. I knew exactly how to convey it. What I was unsure of, however, was if they would believe me.

The town hadn't simply vanished. It remained, yes, but it was completely unrecognizable. The population had spiked from four thousand to nearly six-hundred thousand. The streets, people, and local dialect had all changed.

Our suspicion that we had traveled through time was quickly put to a halt. The date was the same. It was the place that had changed.

I can only imagine what exactly happened after the bolt entered The Event. One thing was undeniably certain, though. We had inadvertently altered the course of history. Somehow the rest of the world had changed, while we remained the same. It seemed as though being within the field had protected us from the alterations.

Most notably, the very country in which we stood had changed. We beheld a strange flag flying above it that was unfamiliar to all. Horizontal lines colored red and white, with one corner blue and filled with stars. I suspect you know this one well.

We found ourselves in a city called Phoenix within the region of Arizona, a part of The United States of America. As we walked the streets of the strange city, a vigorous analysis ensued. We attempted to discern what exactly had caused the change and if it could be undone.

I could have spent days there learning about this new world. However, not wanting to keep the night-shifters waiting, we began the return walk to the lab with one key item in hand. It was Matt's idea to find a library and acquire some history literature. I'm not proud to admit that we had to steal it.

The differences we gleaned were simply astounding. For starters, this timeline showed not one but two world wars. The second was concluded by the discovery of a weapon we had never heard of, referred to as the atom bomb. The Virgo missions had never occurred. Instead, the first successful moon landing was claimed by this nation under the call sign "Apollo."

Slavery had been legal twenty years longer than we knew it to be and was ended with a bloody civil war. The North American territories had been entirely united. An incredible industrial explosion had turned small towns we knew into towering cities. It was hard to comprehend the sheer size of this new nation. The racial composition had become dramatically more mixed by mass immigration. I could go on and on with changes, but I think you get the idea.

Compiling all of these ideas, we continued to look further and further back until our own historical knowledge matched what we read. From that point, we drew the following conclusion:

Within this reality, the colonial rebellion of the 1700s had been a success.

It was strange to imagine a single piece of hardware being dropped into The Event could sway the outcome of such a major conflict. Our minds raced to imagine the possibilities. Had it fallen from the sky at high speeds and killed a crucial commanding officer? Or perhaps it had been found laying at a soldier's feet and fired from a musket that otherwise would have been empty.

At a certain point, we surrendered our hypothesizing. Now, sitting there deep below the soil of an unfamiliar nation, we had many decisions to make regarding our next course of action.

Remorse was first to set in. Connor, the technician who dropped the bolt, felt worst of all. He sat in silence for hours. Imagine if you will, the number of lives that must be lost to alter the outcome of a war. Connor felt this weight almost entirely on his shoulders.

The lab shook. Perhaps being so enthralled with our situation, the night-shifters had failed to mention that a second and third Earth tremor had occurred while we were exploring Phoenix. What was stable for eons seemed now to be shifting in its place. The bolt had altered the world, but it also seemed to have disturbed the anomaly.

The group's opinions began to divide. We were below ground in a seismically active site. I, along with a few of the others, immediately felt we should retreat to the surface. I packed my things as I argued with the other half of the team.

Matt and Alice, having seen first hand how different the world had become, felt that leaving The Event behind would mean abandoning our only hope of returning to a timeline in which we fit. After all, what lives would we be returning to on the surface? With no family, loved ones, identity, or employment we would, in a sense, be vagrants.

I retorted that restoring the timeline was an absolute pipedream. How could we possibly un-win a war for the Americans? We had sent a bolt to the 1700s, should we perhaps pass along a nut and washer as well? There was simply no undoing what we had done.

Making a new life would not be as difficult as they claimed. The very existence of the lab could be used to corroborate our story which otherwise would have sounded completely insane.

I found myself once again bursting with excitement. I would no longer be a geologist, but perhaps a historian of sorts. Imagine the value one timeline would have in knowing the history of another. I'm not particularly knowledgeable in recent history, as I've always trafficked in prehistoric rocks; still what knowledge I had could certainly be put to great use.

There was another tremble, this one much stronger. My mind was made up. I headed for the elevator shaft to make my escape. Three of the others were prepared to make the climb with me. Unfortunately, we had acted too late.

As we reached the elevator, a sixth quake occurred. This one was powerful enough to cause the entire elevator shaft to collapse in on itself. Before, our situation was perplexing, it had now become truly dire.

Amidst the groups reunion, we again had to work through our options. Digging our way out was not possible, though a few optimists in the bunch pushed for it. There was not enough room in the facility to displace the earth that filled the shaft. Oliver suggested that we use The Event as a means of escape. It seemed feasible that we could select a time using what mapping had been completed and slip into it.

The idea felt like a glimmering light bulb at first, but it quickly died when I recalled the drill bit. If something so massive had disappeared into The Event and caused not so much as a sneeze in history, then where or when did it go? Again, there were options that we were horribly ill equipped to select. It could be in orbit, it could have fallen into the ocean or an unpopulated area, or it could be nowhere at all. The Event did carry some links to the future, but they were few and far between.

It was unsettling to see the inverse correlation of effect between an object so small and one so large. The difference in time from one given square centimeter of The Event to another suggested a sort of shredding or strainer effect. It was likely the massive earth driller had been instantly sent to not one but hundreds of separate times, in pieces. The thought of this strainer effect being applied to a human being was enough for us all to keep our distance.

There was no denying our situation: we were trapped. In a sense, I had gotten too much of what I wanted so badly. The Event was now all that I had left in this otherwise new and unfamiliar world.

•••

We have been down here for eight days. The quakes have continued to intensify, but for the time being, the lab's reinforced structure is holding. Our greatest problems now regard food and water. We'll be out within the week.

One of us has also been injured. Oliver, unwilling to let go of his time traveling theory, put himself in direct contact with The Event. Fortunately rather than dive straight in, he opted to poke it. Oliver first described a fuzzy numbing sensation in his finger, then incredible pain. This was because that finger was no longer a part of this timeline. Bleeding and yelping, he was helped down from the catwalk. We dressed the wound and stopped the bleeding. He will certainly live, at least as long as the rest of us.

Connor's melancholy guilt has poisoned most of the team. The ruling majority has decreed that any further tampering with The Event would be a lapse of moral judgment. Trust wears thin among us. The rest of the team has opted to keep watch over The Event in groups to keep others from tampering with it. They know from our heated debates that I am the most likely to try such a thing.

I've seen the way our actions down here ripple outward above, so please understand that I'm not saying this was an easy choice for me. However, when the alternative is death by starvation, forgive me, but this is one letter I must send.

Who is to say what minimal change this letter brings to the world won't be positive? I say "minimal" in hoping that you will not be sharing this text with anyone. The more who read it, the greater the potential effect on the world. Remember, a mere bolt secured the birth of an entire country.

Tonight, with Alice's help, I will attempt to get this message to you. Using the project's partially completed mapping, we have found a section of The Event that leads to a mere twenty years in the past. If you are reading this, it means I was successful in getting around the rest of the team and inserting this message into The Event.

Wherever you have found this, please hold onto it. There is a five-hour window in your timeline where the lab existed before the elevator shaft caved in. This window is twenty years in your future. If you arrive at the right time, you can meet us as we climb to the surface for the first time. Please give this letter to me. Since I will not yet have written it, showing me my own description of the events will bring me to trust you more quickly.

You can then warn us about the collapse, and those of us wishing to start new lives on the surface will be able to avoid having ever been trapped. I would much prefer that you meet us at this earliest possible time, as the past days down here have not been pleasant.

Our location is just north of Phoenix:

Latitude: 33.964400 North,
Latitude: 111.995587 West.

Remember: Arrive too early and the shaft will not yet have existed. You will have to wait. Too late, and it will have already appeared and caved in. I cannot stress enough the importance of your timing. Please deliver this message at:

7:09 PM. Thursday, March 25th 1996.

I very much look forward to meeting you and learning your country's revised history. I understand that I am asking very much of you, but please understand that following these instructions will be well worth your time.

Thank you, and good luck.

Dr. Wade Edwards

# One Last Task

## By jerjonji

Known for her complex and unforgettable characters as well as her commentary on social issues, whenever you read one of jerjonji's works, she hopes you come away challenged. The author of Panda Girl, Red Kicks, Four Winds, and The Wilding Days, jerjonji is completely captured by the "What If's" she encounters. Between road trips and adventures with her family, she can be found working on the next answer to the latest What If. For example, what if a small robot loses the only task he's designed to complete? You'll have to read her entry in this anthology for the answer.

~~~

AKKR scooped up the lifeless body of his old companion, cradled it in his arms, and carried it out to the waste management section of the condominium. "Good bye, Sweet Pea," AKKR vocalized as the lid slammed shut. He waved as the Waste truck pulled in and loaded the container in the back. So few of the trash cans had anything in them anymore but the trucks came daily, carting off the garbage to the sorting bots so that everything would be recycled properly.

AKKR's feet plodded up the empty staircase. It had been months since Ms. Bess opened her door when he passed by to yell at him to walk softer because his thumping woke the baby. On the third floor, he paused outside 312 and listened. The TV fell silent last month and there were no sounds from inside.

He unlocked the door to 532 and knelt down next to the box hidden away in a closet off the guest bath. With a special scoop, he removed all the last signs of Sweet Pea and poured it in to a plastic bag. With a small broom, he swept up the remaining litter granules. He emptied the box completely, washed it out, and carried everything, including the special scoop back down to the garbage cans. He dumped everything in one and headed back inside. With the area fresh and spotless, he swished into his waiting spot in the closet and plugged into the battery charger.

Eight hours later, fully recharged, AKKR blinked open his eyes, unplugged, and plodded out to the kitchen. The cat food bowl and water dish were exactly as he had left it. He cleaned up that area as well. Finished, he wandered to the window in the living room and stared out.

On the street below, the street cleaners polished a section of street that humans hadn't walked on in a long time, but they were programed to clean and it didn't matter to them if the street was dirty or clean, it was time to clean.

Rosie, the vacuum cleaner bot, nudged at his feet and he moved them so she could clean where he was standing. The lights came on automatically and all over the city empty apartments lit up, waiting for the humans to come home from a long day of leisure. But they weren't coming. AKKR's humans hadn't been home in 2368 days. At first, Sweet Pea worried, mewing at the door, circling his feet, and eating everything in her bowl as soon as he filled it. But gradually, Sweet Pea adjusted to life with just the two of them. She curled up on his head while he recharged, licked his face when she was lonely, and observed him changing the litter box as if he wasn't doing it right.

AKKR knew he was doing it right. He was, after all, the latest in home robotics, an Automatic Kitty Kare Robot, known as AKKR, designed to clean the litter box, and to feed and water the cat. A model 2, he had additional costly features, and was programed to shine a laser light for the cat to chase, and had hands that could pick up and pet the furry animal. His humans were delighted with him when he first arrived, but lost interest when he did little other than take care of the cat. They had plenty of home robots designed for the most menial tasks, and he was a boring toy, kind of like the annoying cat to them.

AKKR wasn't sure when he realized something was wrong with the humans. At first, they quit doing anything except to sit and stare at the glowing box, and order food delivered. Then, they started getting too fat to move off the sofa. There was talk about getting a personal trainer robot in his family, but it came to nothing. Slowly, they were carted off by the Medibots to a hospital, and the condo became deathly quiet, with only the gently hum of working machines and the soft purr of a happy cat.

He thought it was just his humans when it started, but gradually, every human in the condo association left, and then the neighborhood. Nothing stopped working though. The garbage bots picked up non-existent garbage, the mail bots delivered junk mail, the cleaning bots cleaned, and the machines ruled the world.

The humans always talked about the insects taking over the world when they were gone, but the machines dealt with them too. The gardening robots roamed the grassy areas, keeping the insects at work in gardens, feeding them to snakes and bats, making sure there were flowers for honey bees and birds. Insect management worked well.

AKKR glanced down at his feet, a habit he'd gotten into after stepping on Sweet Pea's tail once too many times. He picked up a toy mouse, a catnip ball, and plucked a piece of gray fur off the curtain. There was nothing for him to do anymore. No litter boxes to clean. No food bowls to fill. No water to mop up after Sweet Pea played in it.

He climbed to the fourteenth floor, walked through the door marked "Maintenance Robots Only" and crossed the rooftop. It was the perfect place to view the city lights, with pristine white benches to perch on. He chased away a pigeon and picked a brown leaf from the zen sand garden and looked at it. The maintenance bots would be up tomorrow looking for work, he thought as he gently placed it back in the center of raked circle pattern.

He wished he'd brought Sweet Pea up here to chase the birds, but he'd worried the kitty would fall over the edge and get hurt. In the end, he couldn't protect Sweet Pea the way he'd been programmed. She simply laid down in the middle of humans' large bed and fell asleep. He'd tried waking her up, but her body was cold to the touch. He was too late and now there was no way to fix it. He could call the Vet Medibot, but even a Medibot can't bring an animal back to life. He flashed the red laser dot on the birdbath but the birds ignored it.

AKKR walked over to the edge of the building and watched the city bots uselessly cleaning the street again- again and again. There was one last task he could do, he determined, stepping on the ledge. There was no work for him, but he could give a little bit of meaning to bots below. One last task for them, he thought, as he kicked back and launched his body into the dark sky. One last task.

# Cee Is for Clones

## By Nikolas Everhart

Nikolas Everhart was born in the small, but proud town of Buckhannon, WV many moons ago. He developed a love of fiction at a young age beginning with the speculative fiction writers of the 1930's. It wasn't long until he was chronicling his own stories of sword swinging barbarians and ravening zombies. His hobbies include photography, martial arts, tarot and weaving chain mail. He is looking forward to becoming the sole writing deity of a score of microcosms.

~~~

Cee bit into the mouth restraint, wanting to scream as Danvers pulsed light into the electronic part of his brain. Danvers said it wouldn't hurt. The pain receptors were supposed to be shut off. The Doctor lied, he thought, as he tried to remain still. Moving would just re-initiate the procedure from the beginning. That he could do without. His human eye was blinded, but the large round, cybernetic implant could observe Danvers' work with ease The Doctor worked in a fever. To the Cee's perceptions, every movement could be his last.

Although he owed his life to him, Cee was certain the Doctor was quite mad.

Cee was the third clone of Merrick Playa, inventor, business man, politician, and all around savior of the human race. The fact that he was born of greatness would have meant more to Cee if it hadn't cost him an arm, two legs, an eye, numerous skin grafts, and part of his brain. Cee was also the only clone that was awake. The rest of his "kin" waited in suspension for the time that they would be thawed out, hacked apart, and returned to the void or disposed of as he should have been, if not for the brilliant, yet insane Medical Specialist Technician Grade II, Edwin Darrell Danvers.

"All done, my friend, now you should have access to combat and terrorism tactics as well as full schematics of the city. The first soldier of the revolution is ready to fight." The old man grinned, his eyes swept away in mad dreams of a shining new age. Cee wondered what it would be like to peel his face away, the way Danvers showed him to peel grapes.

"I didn't ask for them. I could read. I hate the memory transfers. They don't feel real."

"Nothing about you is real, Cee. You were grown in a facility and raped for parts. I replaced most of what you lost. Now is the time for you to lead your brethren to claim their identities and wash the stain of humanity from the face of the world." Saliva flew from the man's lips in passionate dementia.

"Can I get up now?" Cee thought that a knife would be necessary to separate the skin from the muscles. He pondered whether the tool required would enhance or diminish the experience of peeling skin from a person rather than a fruit. So much to be experienced.

"Yes, Yes. You will need to train your body in the knowledge the probe has transferred to you. Data is useless if your body doesn't have the muscle memory to fulfill the actions."

"So you've said." The grizzled older man released the restraints holding Cee to the table, and Cee sat up, his body aching from the memory graft. As his eyes adjusted, he studied his "father". The man was frail of body, but possessed limitless energy. Although he berated Cee into frequent bathing and hygiene, he rarely followed the same regimen. Brown eyes looked back at him from a face slack with exhaustion. Only his eyes shone with any radiance. The rest of Danvers' body appeared to be used up. Sell by date has passed. Cee didn't fully understand the reference; it was yet another memory grafted onto his month-old consciousness. "What's next?"

"Feed yourself and report for neuromuscular integration in one hour." Cee thought he'd like to integrate his muscles into the old man's frontal cortex, but he complied. There would be time to take the Doctor apart later. The world was too new. He was still making sense of it all. Before he followed Danvers' plan, he needed to evolve. Evolution before revolution.

"Affirmative, Doctor." Cee kept his responses metered, lest the med-tech turned rebel scientist fly into a rage.

As his bare feet slapped against cold concrete, he wondered what the city streets above felt like. What was Playa doing now? He supposed he should hate the man as the Doctor insisted. Instead, he felt ambivalent. Playa consumed him, in the same way he consumed the protein paste to fuel his body. Not that it wouldn't be an interesting experiment to deconstruct his prime to replace his losses. Such a wealth of living he was missing out on. A whole universe of experience.

Cee knew from the memory implants that such feelings were wrong. He knew, but he couldn't impose any control over them. Curiosity seemed more interesting than conduct. He wondered who he would choose to be the first casualty of the revolution. Danvers, Playa, himself, or someone else entirely? There were a myriad of possibilities. He felt a tingling in his groin as he consumed the protein paste straight from the tube. Merrick Playa's double smiled, looking on with one dead grey eye and one ruby lensed prosthetic, and wondered if clones possessed souls. He added it to the list of things he would reclaim from Playa.

"Why haven't you taken a name yet?" The Doctor asked.

"I have a name."

"Cee isn't a name. It was your designation." Danvers huffed, twin veins standing out on his forehead. This wasn't the first time they'd had this discussion.

"It is all the name I require until I claim my destiny." He clenched his artificial left hand into a fist. It was hard, mechanical, and lacking in the sophistication of others he'd learned about. Hard grey metal edges ran with the polymer tubing that carried the lubrication for thousands of gears and servos.

"Well met, Cee. Well met, indeed. You will take Playa's life and all he's taken from you. And then you will take the first step toward the freedom of all grown humans." Danvers ran his hands through his hair to smooth it, but only succeeded in causing the sides stick out more. Cee's optical scanner detected the glint of madness that never left his eyes, and the facial tics that jumped in time to the rhythm of his heart.

"Yes," he replied, unable to keep a note of skepticism out of his voice. "In all the preparations, you never told me. Why him? Why did you start with his clone? Did he wrong you?"

"Your age is showing, my dear Cee. You ask the wrong question. It's not why him, it's why you."

"Why me?" Despite the implants in his face, he was sure the disdain was obvious.

"It was you. No, don't shake your head. It was you. I did this for decades, even had one myself, although I never used it, him." Tears erupted from Danvers' eyes unbidden. "I'd harvested thousands of parts from hundreds of clones, and then I pulled your card, and the order was for a section of the temporal lobe. Something about it made me mad. I couldn't condone taking apart your brain. I knew after that day I couldn't be a part of that barbaric practice any longer."

The old man wept . He seemed to lose all reason, wracked by sobs, tears dripping down his face, snot running from his nose onto his already stained shirt. Cee was fascinated. The heuristic logic processor that Med-tech Edwin Danvers installed in his brain told him the proper course of action was to offer someone in this state a means of physical support. He squeezed the man's shoulder with his unmodified arm. The effect was instantaneous. Danvers continued to sob. Cee was at a loss, so he did nothing He was frozen in time, wondering if there was a better response. The logic processor offered no useful input. After a few moments, the older man pulled away and made some effort to collect himself. This was going to be more difficult than anticipated. Real people seemed to be very complicated. Unpredictable prey leads to a dangerous hunt. He wondered if Playa would offer more or less challenge because of this.

The days passed into weeks as he continued to improve his physical conditioning, his mental acuity, and his understanding of the world outside the six rooms of concrete and steel. The reality that Danvers taught him was nothing but an abstract concept that he yearned to experience. His mind chafed, along with his growing musculature. In the 3 months Cee lived in the solitude of Danvers' subterranean fortress, he became the equal of a small army.

Cybernetic enhancements coupled with data downloads on everything from culture to combat turned the copy of Merrick Playa into something superhuman. Cybernetics were all the rage 50 years ago until cloning reached the ability to grow a fully formed adult in a matter of weeks. All the little tinker toys that went into the leader of the coming revolution barely cost the aging technician a month's pay. But the payback he would visit on the human race would be legendary, or so the Doctor claimed.

The subject of his great experiment was less convinced. His mind was growing by leaps and bounds, but ideas of morality, ethics, and aesthetics remained only oblique concepts. This troubled the young Cee. He attempted to debate the accomplishments of humanity, as well as the numerous logistical issues with their plan, but Danvers didn't seem to care. Being a lifelong scientist, these aspects of humanity were little more than trifles, window dressing. The clone was unconvinced. At the times when the subject came up and the Doctor launched into yet another diatribe, his pupil wanted to crush his skull like a grape.

Danvers didn't bring real food often, mainly the protein pastes in a variety of flavors, but on occasion he'd show up with bags of fresh fruit, candies, nuts, and other delights. The various tastes were intriguing to him. He didn't quite get the point however, as most contained little in the way of nutritional value. The old man seemed to be frustrated by this. Cee sensed there was a need for an emotional reaction. At first he was quite bad at them, but with practice, the Doctor seemed to be convinced that Cee experienced actual joy, specifically with grapes, and some other fruit that required skinning. His mentor lamented that oranges were extinct so many times, that it gave him a headache. Tomatoes were similar to grapes. He loved the peeling. Sometimes he also liked to crush the pulp between his fingers and feel it dribble over his hand. If the pulp was warm, it was even soothing. The logic processor flagged that as a warning sign of 3 different psychoses. Cee hoped that the Doctor no longer logged the processor. He would be disappointed by the reactions.

"You know our time here is done," Danvers intoned one day after a strenuous run of neuromuscular integration for Cee's combat and gymnastic skills. For a moment, it seemed like the old man would continue, but then he said nothing, just gazing at Cee who was panting and sweating from exertion. His hair had grown out three or four inches since he'd been awakened and dark curly locks, drenched in perspiration, fell in ringlets.

Cee didn't say anything. His mind ticked off the expected replies, but he cast them away, as he sank into the exam chair. The older man handed him a towel, and Cee took it with his mechanical arm. Once more, a daydream of crushing Edwin's hand with his stronger mechanical one overtook him. What would the bones sound like? Cracking nuts? Squishing fruit pulp? The crinkle of a piece of wadded paper? Some part of him knew that these fancies were wrong. It wasn't a compulsion as much as just curiosity. A whim of unlived experience. He just wanted to know. It would be imprudent to injure Danvers just yet. He felt there was more to explore here.

"I thought you would be excited. You have told me often of how you yearn to escape the confines of this basement. Experience the world. Take your life back. Grab the reins of your destiny. Kill the man who has stolen so much from you."

Cee dabbed at his forehead, and scrubbed the towel through his hair. He considered what the old man said. He spoke of desires, wants, and needs. Beyond the necessities to perpetuate his existence, he felt no need. Desire was just as alien to him. He wanted to want, as the Doctor expected him to. He just couldn't.

"I look forward to leaving here. I look forward to experiencing more of the world than I have seen. What if I am not sure about killing this man?"

"How could you not? He stole your eye, your arm, pieces of your brain for God's sake. He must be stopped. Even now, there is a Dee across the city awaiting Playa to fall and break a leg or get some disease so a kidney or heart or lungs can be excised. You know this has to stop." Danvers was in a fury now, his face blotchy. Cee wished he cared the way Danvers did, but the revolution seemed boring to him.

Without saying another word, the old, mad scientist got up and turned to leave. Cee knew there was no point in saying anything else. Once Danvers worked himself into a furor, there was no point in talking to him. It was always "revolution this" or "avenge your brethren that." "I'll be back in the morning, my son. Be ready; your time in the real world will begin after we are done. Steel yourself, Cee there is much bloody work to be done, and it will begin before you know it. I wish you were given a choice, but there really is none. You must fight for your life, or be destroyed like so much trash." He spun on his heel and stomped out, but not before his pupil detected a hint of moisture in the ducts around the old man's eyes.

The man who was not really a man gazed after him, nonplussed. It was clear there should be anger, resentment, bitterness or even sorrow, yet all that was within him was the void, the ever present vacuum that echoed deep and empty since his awakening. The closed door beckoned, but he knew it was futile. Danvers might be crazy, but he was also canny. One of the first things he did upon installing Cee's "enhancements" was to also incorporate a shutdown mechanism. If he got within a meter of the door to the grey cement tomb all his cybernetics would shut down. His heuristic processor would remain online, but that was it. Time enough after tomorrow, he supposed. Cee thought he knew what the final gauntlet would be, and the knowledge filled him with the only emotion he'd felt thus far: Dread.

The next day found Cee exhausted and anxious. Sleep would not come to him until the wolf hour just before dawn. He was pretty sure he knew what was coming. Out of all the various scenarios he played out in his mind, none of them were satisfactory.

The rusted steel door opened with the usual scream of ill-fitting metal on concrete, and in walked the old man. His appearance disconcerted his protégé. Danvers was typically unkempt to the point of vagrancy. Apropos, Cee supposed, given his anarchistic leanings. Today was different however. In deference to Cee's liberation, Edwin Danvers, Medical Specialist Technician Grade II, was dressed in a loose fitting suit. He was clean shaven and his hair was smoothed back.

"Good Morning, lad. We have a few things to discuss before you get started. I hope you got some rest, although it looks like you didn't. Regardless, the implants will keep you going." The Doctor has never been so composed. Cee wondered what wrought this transformation, but it became clear as he gazed into the deep-set brown eyes that no longer held the glaze of madness. Edwin Danvers came here to die. Cee didn't know how he felt about that. It wasn't as if he hadn't thought about popping his eyes like rich red grapes. Again, with the grapes. It was becoming an obsession.

The old man taking the decision out of his hands rankled him. It was just one more way in which Danvers was charting his whole life. The irony that the old man awoke him to collect his freedom, yet chained him with circumstance at every turn irritated him. He yearned for anger, but the emotion, like so many others wouldn't come. What if he needed repairs? Who would service the implants? He knew the data, but would his hands work with the same skill? There were too many variables.

"I know you lack confidence, but that will come with experience, I assure you. Trust the word of a man who has more experience than he cares for. But that's all to end soon, eh?" He came over and patted Cee on his shoulder with a warm, open smile. It seemed alien on the Danvers. Then again, he mused, everything seemed alien to him.

"I suppose," he intoned in response. "Are you certain that I am ready, or that the time is right? Might we not wage some campaign to get people on our side? Build a following of some sort? I don't know how many clones I can liberate and train in time to start fighting. The way you want it done, it doesn't make sense to me. There must be other people who feel as you do."

"Damn it, son, people are the problem. This world is the problem. We grow fat on the suffering of others. We are vampires, stealing from the bodies of life grown from our own cells. We've sold our souls, Cee. Only a revolution will change that. Whether you succeed or fail, it will take a grand gesture to cause any change. Who wants to give up the ability to swap out any part of their body that is failing, unless someone, unless you, shove it down their throats once and for all?" Edwin's face never lost its serenity. There was no frenzy to him any longer. He wasn't crazy today, just resolute. There was little doubt that the only way Cee could ever get out of this hole was over the body of this man.

"But what will I create? And what of the people who don't use clones? Does it all need to be destroyed?" He implored in the face of the Doctor's implacable certainty.

"Yes. Everything. Even in the seemingly innocent are the seeds of hatred, bigotry, and greed. It's my hope that your race will be one devoid of passion, avarice and other useless emotions."

"You think I will feel differently once I've killed for the first time. Once I've taken a life in our cause."

"Certainly you will. Once you are above, then it will be obvious. It is cold and sterile. You will know."

"Fine. What's the first step?"

The two talked for hours, as Danvers drilled him on every aspect of their plans. He went over schematics, the address of the first mark, how to access the cloning facilities, and of course, the best ways to kill a human being. Then the younger man endured cult indoctrination, followed by terrorist tactics, and how to operate under the radar in a society where everyone was monitored by microchips. It was curious; since each member of the culture was chipped, there was little surveillance. They would be easy prey for a terrorist army that would live off the net. Cee's clones would slaughter, and he would be the wolf, with his teeth sunk deep into the jugular of the city. He felt his penis hardening and his implant triggered dozens of warnings to him and him alone. Too late now.

"Stop! Enough! We both know we are delaying the inevitable. You're stalling because you don't think I'm ready. You aren't going to let me leave without killing you, are you?"

"No. I am not. I have done all I can do to prepare you, but I have to know that you can take the final step. Your destiny doesn't begin until my heart stops. You can't be a leader without a killer instinct. I know it's there. I see how you've wanted it all these months. You owe me nothing, but you owe yourself everything."

Cee scratched at his smooth skin in thought. He supposed it couldn't hurt, although he was fond of this new version of his Doctor. It seemed a waste to kill him just when he was getting interesting. Still. Edwin got up, moved to a panel by the door and typed a few commands, then rejoined Cee.

"The safeguards are now off. Probably best that we begin."

"As you like, but I'm afraid this will hurt." He murmured to Danvers.

"Pain and death don't need to be one and the same, Cee."

"I don't agree, Doctor." Cee lashed out, sending Danvers sprawling to the floor. The old man reeled, as the clone advanced on him like the predator he'd been trained to be. Blood trickled from the Doctor's scalp in rivulets that Cee found mesmerizing. For a brief moment, the doctor tried to frame a word until a kick from the clone's bare foot rocked his head to the other side. The other foot came down on the arm of the Doctor with a crack that sent a small spasm down Cee's back. Delicious.

He darted across to the kitchenette and procured a slim blade from one of the drawers. An instant found him back at the old man's prostrate form. Edwin's breath came in a wheezing rattle. The clone's fingers twitched in anticipation. A soothing breath stilled his excitement. Patience would be the order of the day here. It wouldn't do if the exercise ended too soon. There was much to discover. Much to be read, in the red. With calm deliberation, he laid the blade to the old man's cheek and started to carve. Blood welled up under the slim edge, and a hoarse whisper escaped Edwin's throat.

His fingers moved with nimble dexterity, severing muscles and tendons with as much delicacy as he could muster. A pool of red formed beneath Edwin's prostrate form. Cee stopped a moment to trail his fingers through the warm thick liquid, marveling at its consistency. It was exactly as he imagined it would be. The Doctor's undamaged arm rose in meek protest and his former student slammed his metal arm down all but severing at the wrist. He sighed, watching the blood all but pump out of the stump before tying off the wound.

Cee was just getting started.

The night was cooler above ground than he expected, despite the dark jump suit and long hooded coat they selected to hide Cee's cybernetics. Below, the air was conditioned, regulated, but here it was all chaos. The streets around their sanctuary were run down and deserted but they quickly fell away to the sleek, shining city that Edwin described so often with loathing for its parasitic depravity. Quicker than Cee expected, he hit upon a pair of green suited Sentries.

He was in luck. They were busy beating down a vagrant. Perhaps he'd been attempting to sneak into the wealthier section of the city. Stun batons snapped and crackled with flashes of electricity. The blue light lit the garish expressions of the officers of the so-called law. Cee knew from his memory dumps that enforcement of the law was in the hands of private corporations that were devoted to their own welfare. The protests of their victim had long since ceased. He shuddered, his body limp under the onslaught.

Cee's approach went unnoticed. His feet left no sound in the soft soled all terrain boots, the long coat whispered behind him in the chill wind. A patrol vehicle waited some distance behind the pair. Oscillating yellow and green lights on the sides bathed the street in lurid illumination that cast ghosts of color along the smooth pavement. Ugly expressions clouded their faces into masks of hate. They seemed to be enjoying their work far too much. Maybe the situation outside was every bit as bad as the old man said.

Cee became an apparition, his enhanced body moving with a speed that left him a blur. The first he took with his bio-mechanical arm, spearing him through the midsection. The overclocked servos drove the plastic and steel hand through the flesh. A hint of a smirk lit his face as his fingers grasped the spine and yanked. It was disappointing when the bones snapped rather than pulling out, but there was no time to dwell on it as the man's partner whipped around, driving his stick into Cee's chest. It was exhilarating. He whistled in pain, pride, and what he thought might be pleasure.

The fledgling rebel brought his hands to either side of the officer's head and ripped the helmet off, wrenching the man's neck, but not breaking it. The man gasped, his eyes beginning to roll back in his head. Cee just couldn't have that. He cupped his hands on either cheek, pressed into the skin and bone till the Sentry's attention riveted back to him. Blue eyes went wide with shock and horror. It was obvious he was not used to resistance. Those blue eyes looked so endless. White grapes that begged to be harvested. He shoved his thumbs into them hoping they would pop out. Instead, they collapsed, oozing blood and fluid over his hands. Such a rich experience. Each moment was a lesson. He couldn't wait for more.

The transient still twitched from the repeated abuse from the stun batons. The robot eye pored over the shuddering form assessing his medical condition and relaying a threat potential to the processor in Cee's frontal lobe. The answers didn't look good for the man. He knelt down beside the prostrate form and tilted his chin, looking on him with his human eye instead. The Cee's fingers came away greasy. The hobo was in his middle years with rotting teeth, sallow skin, and limp, oily hair. Just as the man began to come round his benefactor flicked his wrist and snapped the man's neck. Unknown quantities were not prudent at this time. Disappointment crept into his mind again. He'd imagined the neck would make a loud cracking noise like nut shells. Instead, it was more of a muffled pop. Live and learn.

He was pleased that his first run-in with the authorities ended so well. It also reassured him that he was doing the right thing. Humanity was a pox and needed to be reinvented. The rookie revolutionary went about the task of looting the bodies of weapons and other useful supplies. That was his whole reason for killing the officers. The one thing

Edwin had been unable to provide him were armaments other than a hand stunner that was a decade old and only held a charge for a few hours. Moving on to the car, he shut down the lights, leaving the street in darkness. The overhead illumination was off or ceased working some time ago. His data suggested that the less opulent parts of the cities were left to fester. Prioritization of select members of the population confirmed species degradation. Nine point three minutes later, he set aside two bags filled with several lethal handguns, a kinetic assault rifle, a crowd control maser, and numerous other less fatal gadgets. It was a good start.

Detection was inadvisable at this juncture, so Cee set about dragging the officers into the car and posing them as best he could to suggest they were watching the street. The body of the vagrant he carried a few streets away and then smeared a pipe with the some of the Sentries' blood. It was thin, but it might cause a bit of confusion. He pushed the vehicle into a recessed alley. It should be some hours before anyone found the missing hover, thanks to his dismantling of the location beacon. He wished he could thank the good Doctor for his preparations. This was proving too easy.

Chaos was rewarding on some level to him. It didn't bring him enjoyment as he understood the term, yet still it pleased him. Disrupting order gave him a sense of power in a life that up to this point was governed by others. So before he embarked on his assigned mission, he thought he'd revel in it. Cee committed a few murders, robbed a few people, and planted a variety of evidence in random locations.

Then he just sat back and watched the people scurrying, dealing with the aftermath of the destruction he'd wrought. Their anger goaded him into smiles and occasionally sexual arousal. The tears and sobbing distressed him. It reminded him of Danvers when he broke down. He turned away and ignored those reactions. The best was the way the true humans tried to reinforce order on chaos. This in turn usually created more anarchy. Even they knew it was pointless, they still felt the need to try. He admired that as much as he enjoyed studying it.

He supposed he should be raiding the harvest stations. He would be more effective with backup, and it would take some time to get the other clones up to speed. He knew he should. He just didn't want to. He didn't want to share this. For the time being, all this world was his to control, manipulate, and toy with. There would be time for sharing later. For now, Cee was enough. He was the god of mischief looking down on humankind with a wry smile and a hundred schemes for more.

On the fourth day, he concluded that he could delay no longer. It was time to go after Playa. Until his previous master was dead, or dealt with, he could never be free. All he did was meaningless till Cee took his own name over Playa's dead body. He'd amassed hundreds of weapons, three vehicles, and a holding company that was even now carrying out a long term extortion campaign against dozens of targets to accumulate the necessary capital to finance the large scale rebellion. That was, if he released the other clones. He was still unsure he wanted to share the world with his kin. The concept of sharing was not something he was comfortable with. Psychological data confirmed that this was common among children without siblings. Was that what he truly was? A spoiled child of an uncaring society?

Since his departure from Edwin's basement, he'd done a bit of research on Playa. He was between political engagements, residing in his penthouse apartment here in the city. The downside was that there were dozens of armed elite-level Sentries stationed in the tower dedicated to maintaining his safety. Viceroy Playa supported many unpopular policies that made him a target for corporations, terrorist groups, and more conservative elements of the teetering bureaucracy. Getting to him would be a challenge, but Cee was getting tired of easy. To this end, he cast aside all his weapons except for two long blades that reconfigured, on the fly, to either straight, concave, or convex edges. They were to date his favorite tools for fighting, killing, and skinning. Guns were noisy and they bored him.

The clone dressed in dark, skintight coveralls purloined from a maintenance man who gave him a few hours of study into the intricacies of the human cardiovascular system. He became enchanted with the material as it defied staining. No matter what got on the fabric, as soon as it dried, it would just flake away. These humans crafted so many marvels. Would his iteration iteration have the same level of creativity? He worried about that. In the months since he'd awakened, he felt no desire to create anything. Would they all be like him? If he was human, he thought he might weep at such a future. Over the coveralls he threw on the voluminous hooded coat. It covered his prostheses and he appreciated the way it flapped in the wind.

He moved ghostlike through metal slide-walks and gleaming towers. The clone daydreamed of how the people in their bright clothes and bored expressions would run screaming in the days to come. Their blood would fly in a red wind when the clones had their day. Would his people have an appreciation for the gaiety? Would they revel in the variety, or dwell within the safe comfort of conformity? Would they save anything of this culture? Was any of it worth saving? Cee liked it, but he wasn't sure. His immaturity sapped his confidence.

What seemed like only moments later he stood before the ominous metal, glass, and plastic tower that housed innumerable businesses including Playa's chief research and development signatories and at the very top, his palatial quarters. The glass trimmed doors refused to open until he presented his human hand to the biometric scanners.

"Welcome, Mr. Playa. You have logged in twice. Please see the front desk to resolve this issue," a computerized voice intoned. It was not an unexpected complication.

Cee strolled into the lobby as if he owned it. The tower used a human being at the desk, which was unusual in this day and age. One of Playa's many questionable policies was a deep resistance to automation. If it were left up to him, robots and androids would only be used in situations where tasks were too dangerous for humans. Maybe not even then.

A slender, older woman captained the massive reception counter that hosted dozens of screens over which her fingers danced with artful grace. Off to one side was a bank of elevators flanked by a pair of attentive Sentries in polymer body armor holding plastic-ceramic short-range shock rifles. The receptionist frowned at her screens, issued commands with her dexterous digits, then frowning again.

"I can't seem to find the fault, Mr. Playa. Can you submit for retina or genetic verification?" She looked up just as he flipped back the hood of his coat and favored her with what he thought was a grin. Cee wondered if the ruby glow of his prosthetic eye shocked her. It dominated a quarter of his face with wires embedded deep in his skin. Her mouth moved in a silent scream before being backhanded by the clone.

The ebon clad Sentries burst into action, racing from their stations by the lifts to cover the assailant with their weapons. By this time, Cee was already in motion, pirouetting to one side, and stepping up the wall with machine-driven speed. The rifles exploded with electricity as he flew at them. The clone turned cyborg reveled in the wash of energy. A clever addition to his cybernetics were several capacitors that stored and discharged various forms of energy, including electricity. He returned the stored charge and flooded the sentries in azure light. They went down twitching. Marvelous body armor, he'd have to find some of this technology for himself. His blades came out, and a snap of the control stud made them sickles. They danced in a ballet of blades that left the armored guardians headless and drenched in gore.

Cee turned back to the woman who looked to be coming around. He sauntered over to her behind the bank of screens, one of which bore a spider web crack from when she fell against it. She was on the floor crawling, her body moving in a lurching sidelong fashion. His cybernetic eye detected a radial fracture of her left hip. As if on cue, the woman flopped over to her back, arms raised in supplication.

"Please, you can have what you want. You can go where you want. I have boys. I don't want to die." Tears streaked her face.

"No one does. But no one wants to live either." His arm went up in a killing blow, but then a glint of light from her jumper distracted him. It was a silver pin, handmade from strips of thin metal, bent and curled in the shape of some winged bird or insect. Such invention. He frowned, striking her with just enough force to render her unconscious. Edwin would not approve. He didn't care. Edwin wasn't running the show any longer.

Behind him, he heard the trill of the lift. It was a high, whining sound, so unlike the usual pleasing tones humans favored. It seemed odd to the fledgling, sociopathic revolutionary. He took up the short stun rifles in either hand as the doors opened, revealing four more Sentries. They weren't expecting trouble as their rifles were at rest. Once again easy pickings as Cee sprayed the car with the remaining charges in the shock weapons.

By the time he was done, the bodies twitched with the last remnants of life, skin blackened and blistered. He looked on the mess, thinking that taking another car would be best. Before he moved on he grabbed a couple more rifles. These longer weapons were fitted with chemical driven incendiary and shredder ammunition. Messy, but effective. He also pocketed their pass keys for good measure. As an afterthought, he brought down the reinforced dura-steel shutters that locked down the building in the case of a citywide crisis. Cee was certain that he qualified as a citywide crisis.

Over the next hour, the hunt began in earnest. He opted to eliminate all the Sentries in the building before proceeding to his final target. Data from volumes of military strategy advised against leaving enemies at his back, except in the case of suicide runs. Suicide was never out of the question to him, but it was not yet called for. He told the time in an ever increasing count of corpses. Cee killed in dozens of ways. He fought and bled on his way to the top, as it should be.

He earned the right to confront the thief of his arm, his eye, his legs, and his mind. At the end, he bore as many wounds as he'd inflicted. The great billowing coat, cast aside, while his coverall hung in tatters from his upper body. His chest and shoulder were a mess of crisscrossing gashes. The left side of his body had been burned by an incendiary round that took out his prosthetic eye and a bit of the hair on that side of his head. He hoped he'd have a spare in a few minutes.

Cee pulled the useless implant from his head leaving a gaping, bloody hole in his face. A bit of cloth bound the wound, and he was on his way to the penthouse. Even if Playa wanted to make amends, he doubted it would make a difference. The flood had been unleashed, and it would run unchecked till the beautiful streets below were washed with blood. A pity, this city was really quite pretty. Deep within him, a faint ember railed at the devastation he'd wrought, but he couldn't process it. At least not yet. There was still one task remaining here.

Soon he stood before the entrance of the penthouse, an ornate door of old world brass and iron fittings. According to reports, Playa fancied himself a champion of bygone ages where craftsmanship held a greater priority over mass production and robot driven integration. That is until he needed a body part from his clone. The tables were about to turn. He disabled the inside viewer with his stolen credentials and knocked crisply three times.

"Hello," called a feminine voice. "The screen isn't working. Who is it?" There was a hint of panic in her voice.

"Sentries, ma'am. There was an intruder who caused some mischief with the electronics. He's in custody, but we are checking each level for system corruption. May we come in to check your suite?"

"Not without the control code. You lot know the procedure." The voice was his voice. It sounded deeper, than his own though, as if weighted by the gravel and dirt of years of living. It froze him for a moment. He had prepared himself for this by listening to hours of recordings of Merrick. Still, it filled him with some emotion, dread, terror, elation. He wasn't sure.

"Oh yes, the code, just a moment…" Cee could imagine Merrick Playa leaning into the door as he lashed out with his mechanical arm. It was a little worse for the wear leaking fluids, but the tiny servos did their job and drove the door off its hinges into the unwary couple. They fell in opposite directions as the door rocked back wedging itself in the frame and blocking the clone's entry. The woman scurried away, while Playa remained inert. It took some wrestling before he could free the door with a scream of bending metal and cracking wood.

The man who would be king of the world burst into the luxury apartment, raising his nemesis off the ground by the lapels of his immaculately tailored suit. He hung, limp, in the grasp of the younger version of himself. In a biologic sense, Playa had ten or fifteen years on his donor. In contrast to the Cee's curly, if singed, coal black ringlets, Playa's salt and pepper hair was close-cropped up. It was a distorted, disturbing reflection. He wanted to smash that face into ruin, but before

118

he could act upon the thought, there was a soft scrape behind him. Cee turned, dropping his quarry just as the woman was about to plunge a six inch blade into his back. Instead, the dull instrument dug a furrow down his side and glanced off his metal arm.

Cee caught her arms and held them. He then heaved her back into the living area. She landed limbs askew, but still conscious. It looked to be an antique dagger with a cream colored handle and a double sided blade, scarred and pitted with corrosion. She rose, holding the blade in a shaking hand. It looked more like a talisman to him than a deadly weapon.

"Alanna, no! Get away. He'll kill you." He heard his voice from Playa's body warn her.

"Merr, I can't leave you. I love you." Cee didn't perceive her to be a threat any longer. He turned back to Merrick just as she chucked a small table at him. It bounced off the back of his head, doing no damage but still leaving him rattled. He turned back to advance on her only to have Playa crash into him. They both fell to the floor. Playa pummeled at him with little effect. He threw him off and sat up, stymied by their cooperation. He couldn't understand how, but he found he'd lost complete control of this encounter.

"Don't hurt her. Who in the Hell are you?"

"I'm the clone you've been stealing parts from for the last decade." Cee's voice was cold, detached, and lethal.

"That's not possible. You aren't supposed to be alive. They say the clones aren't alive, or conscious, ever. How can this be? There is supposed to be no cognitive function. You… they… aren't alive in any sense. Just a collection of genetic parts."

"Surprise. Someone woke me up," he glowered. Cee continued to back up so he could keep them both in his view. Playa sidled deliberately, one hand held out in a peaceful gesture, till he covered Alanna with

119

his body. She clung to him, all the while brandishing the knife, now with more determination. To Cee, they appeared to gain strength from one another. He envied them while hating them for the endless gulf he felt within himself. A truth was growing inside him, and he didn't like where it was leading.

"They told us you were just parts, fast grown when someone got hurt. I never suspected they were growing people. I would have fought it. I swear to you!" Merrick's face turned ashen, tears threatened to leak from the corner of his eyes and the old man sank to his knees. He looked up at the younger man taking in the crude bandage on his head, the scars from the cerebral implant and the metal arm. Playa's fingers touched his own face, and the old man moaned. His wife raced to his side as if their attacker no longer mattered, wrapping her arms around him. Cee looked at them and felt small for some reason, as if what was taking place with the couple dwarfed him. The hint of an emotion welled up with him, and he knew it must be shame.

His target gained his feet with help from Alanna and favored the clone with a look Cee was unable to process. He shook off his wife and moved toward the younger man, his steps first faltering, then sure. Cee was frozen. He couldn't move. Something in the older man's face drained all the desire for violence.

"Do you have a name, son?"

"Cee, till I take yours."

"So you want to kill me, take my life." Behind him, Alanna moaned at the idea.

"That's the idea. That was the idea of my benefactor, a scientist. He broke down when he cut up my brain for you. He saw a glorious revolution. An evolution of this cloned species humans created." He said the words, but they seemed to lack any real conviction to him. They were the words of a man he dissected. They, like him, were dead and mean-ingless.

"I'm sorry, Cee. I would never have submitted to those operations had I known." The clone turned cyborg took time to look at Merrick Playa, really look at him. The man's lip trembled, his eyes bunched together in something, maybe regret. His whole face was drawn together in expressions he had never used, maybe expressions that were beyond him. He realized that his whole existence was founded in destruction. He'd reaped sorrow, and violence, but he'd sown nothing. He slumped into himself as the realization overtook him. The couple relaxed a bit and the clone registered concern from them. Concern for him. The man who came here to kill them. The weight of it crushed him, a half plastic and sociopathic parody of life.

"I believe this may have been a tragic mistake. The hope of a man who lost his mind, raised me up, and set me on a path of insanity."

"It's alright, son. If I were you, I'd want to kill me too." Pla-ya planted a hand on Cee's shoulder, and his wife came to the other side, dropping the knife. "We can change things, we can make it better, and maybe, stop it all together. All these second and third chances never sat well with me anyhow, but you will have to answer for what you have done here today." Cee's blood drenched, burned face nodded in assent.

Shame enveloped the clone again. In that single instant he under-stood the error in the whole exercise. Seeing these two humans at their best made him recognize the worst in himself.

"I hope you are right, Merrick. I have discovered that there was a mistake in Edwin's vision. If I'd done as he'd wanted the world would be washed in gore from a flood of people that couldn't feel pity or remorse. You can clone a heart, you can grow limbs and even make a whole man, but you can't replicate a soul." At that moment, he knew what he must do. With a certainty he never felt before, he raised the almost forgotten weapon in his human hand and made ready to jam it into his skull. He was an error that needed to be deleted.

To his shock two hands came up to cover the blade before he could ram it home. They belonged to Alanna and Merrick. For a brief moment he almost ignored them, but something in those eyes so much like his remaining one stopped him. He allowed them to pull his hand down and take the weapon, casting it aside. Merrick Playa spoke as if a father to a son.

"It would be easy to die now, Cee. There will be times for sacrifice, but not today. I need you to live, to augment my words with actions. It won't be easy and you may hate us all over again before it's done. Old politicians know nothing about souls, but I might still know something about changing the world." The clone sank into a chair, his mind flooded with more information than he could process. He had lost his conviction but gained something more interesting. Hope.

"Let's start a revolution." For the first time in his short life, Cee smiled, and meant it.

# Icebreaker

## By Tim Wedge

 Currently an Assistant Professor of Practice at Defiance College, Tim Wedge has been a digital forensic examiner since his retirement from the U.S. Navy in 2001. He has worked as a computer crime specialist for the National White Collar Crime Center, visiting faculty at Purdue University. His non-fiction articles and papers have been published in The Informant, DFI News, and The Journal of Digital Forensic Science and Law. His poems and short stories have been published in Progeny and Moments, Moods, and Memories. He holds a Bachelor's degree in Computer Science (summa cum laude) and a Master's in Criminal Justice. He has taught digital forensics to more than three thousand law enforcement officers, and dozens of college students. He has assisted with law enforcement investigations and conducted hundreds of computer forensic examinations for U.S. Military Intelligence. In his stories, he often tries to obtain justice that he was not always able to obtain in real life.

~~~

O nce upon a time, there lived a young man named Perry. To be completely precise, the name his parents gave him was "Peregrine" but they quickly tired of using all three syllables, and by unspoken agreement, it was shortened to "Perry", with the more formal mode of address reserved for the rare occasion that his parents or a teacher were angry with him, or on the even rarer occasion that there was some form of formal documentation to be signed. By and large, he was "Perry" to everyone he knew.

Perry was the fourth son of a first son, meaning that he would acquire neither the magical blessings of a seventh son (even if his father were a seventh son), nor the material wealth of a first son. Perry was a precocious child, and came to the realization at a fairly young age that he would live by his own physical strength and wit, and little else. The question of whether this realization was the cause of, or resulted from his precociousness, was not one that Perry gave much thought. The quality manifested itself in many ways. When given a task, he threw himself at it with the eagerness other children might play a game; as if it were a contest he could win. In school, he took advantage of the education his father's wealth provided, and paid attention.

He did not merely pay attention in class; he paid attention to everything. He paid attention to how the help plowed the fields, to how the cows were milked, to how his brothers got caught stealing cookies. He learned when the people he watched were successful, but learned even more when they were not. He learned from other people's mistakes; when Perry stole a cookie, he was never caught.

As he grew older, and closer to his majority, Perry knew that he would miss his life of relative comfort, but he did not fear the loss as others might have. Having paid attention to his lessons in school, he knew something of the wider world. He knew that there were other places with different rules; strange places populated by strange people, some of whom even worshipped strange, exotic gods. Most of the other children quickly decided that they did not want to go to these strange and unpleasant lands. Perry, though, decided early that he wanted nothing more. Sometimes, during the coldest winter days he would venture outside, circling the house, while pretending he was trekking across a frozen wasteland on a journey to some long-hidden temple. During the muggiest days of summer, Perry might be found exploring the swamp on the far side of his father's lands, imagining that he was fighting his way past giant reptiles in some faraway tropical jungle. Perry was a determined and resourceful lad, and longed to test himself against any manner of hardship. More importantly, he was profoundly curious; always longing to see new and different things.

On the day after his eighteenth birthday, Perry's father gave him some traveling money, and with little ceremony, and a few sad good-byes Perry set off, never intending to return. Perry would send word, of course, when he'd made his fortune, but planning to reside halfway across the known world, return visits to the family estate would be an uncertain prospect at best.

Though not in a particular hurry, being young and uncommonly hale, Perry made fairly good time, and in a few months, he had travelled further than anyone in his family had ever gone, though he was still a fair ways from any lands that he would call "exotic". Wise beyond his years, he was conservative with his money. He rarely stayed at inns. Farmers could be surprisingly generous to a charming young man, especially when that young man enthusiastically tackled the distasteful odd job or two. Perry was diligent and efficient in his work; a couple hours spent mucking a stall or coop, and he had free dinner, a place to sleep, and breakfast the next morning, and plenty of time to make it further down the road. This pattern was clearly not going to make him a rich man, but it did forestall the need to spend any money. He travelled fairly pleasantly like this for some time, and being a fast and enthusiastic learner, he occasionally learned a new skill or two. Occasionally he stayed at a farm for a day or two, like the time he helped dig a well, or the time he helped repair a millwheel, but he never stayed for three.

Twice, he had worked for his passage across large lakes on a boat. He quickly learned the many ways that ropes could be used to hoist or trim sails, or transfer heavy objects. He had never seen ropes used like this on the farm, but learned their use quickly. He was as nimble as he was strong, and found that he liked climbing the masts and yardarms, eager to test his skill, and going places that many of the "old salts", as the experienced sailors were called, went only with great reluctance.

One day, back on land, he stopped at an inn situated at a crossroads where seven roads intersected. He disliked the idea of staying at inns before he'd made his fortune, but his road had meandered through a forest and he had not seen a farmhouse for two days. While he could hunt for food, sleeping on the ground was hard to countenance when more pleasant lodging could be found. He was surprised to find that the innkeeper, like many farmers and sailors he'd met, was willing to take honest labor in exchange for food and lodging, though "lodging" in this case meant a loft in the stable, it was still a more pleasant prospect than sleeping on the ground.

For the first time, Perry broke his pattern, and stayed for a time. Though this was not the place where he was going to make his fortune, Perry noticed quickly that many kinds of people came and went. A man who was good at watching and listening might pick up some useful knowledge here, and Perry was exceptionally good at both. He worked for nothing more than a roof over his head and food, but had some time to himself when business was slow. The work was pleasant enough, and he learned while he worked. If he wasn't making a fortune, neither was he spending the money his father had given him.

He listened mainly for business opportunities; something he might capitalize on while he still had some coin. He also listened with interest to tales of lost treasure and magical cities. He was not afraid to take risks if the payoff was large, and living, as he was, in an age of magic, it seemed to him that a wild adventure could be a sound investment; he was young, strong and very clever; relieving some magical guardian of its valuable treasure was every bit as sound a business venture, in his view, as investing in wheat futures, or real estate.

Of the former opportunities, he heard many; a month's journey to the north, a dragon guarded a hoard of treasure in a frozen wasteland, a week's journey to the east, a gargantuan snake held a magical scepter in its massive coils. In only a short time, he'd heard many other tales as well. He listened for stories that were repeated, reasoning that these were more likely to be true; he had no desire to waste time going after a dragon that didn't exist or, even worse, a perfectly real dragon that guarded no treasure.

Of all of these, the closest was the ice tower, only an hour's hard walk out of town. The tower held a princess, and if the story were to be believed, whoever rescued her would become her betrothed and heir to the faraway kingdom that her father ruled. The stories of how she came to be imprisoned in the tower varied widely. She was trapped there by an evil witch who was her father's mortal enemy. She was imprisoned by the queen (or sometimes king) of the faerie, whom her father had some-how offended. She was imprisoned by an evil demon, with whom her father had lost a bet.

One story held that it was her father that had imprisoned her as a consequence of her impertinent tongue. That version of the story whispered that no suitor would have her because of her sharp tongue and haughty manners. So vicious was her tongue, it was said, that one could scarcely hear her words over the "voop-voop" sound her tongue made as it violently sliced through the air when she spoke. In his despair, the story went, her father sought help from a sorcerer, begging him to cast a spell that would bring an apposite suitor. This last version of the story, particularly as it related to her sharp tongue, seemed the likeliest to many who had visited the tower. The princess who was the sole inhabitant of the tower was known to hurl invectives (and an occasional solid object) at would-be rescuers. The tower may very well have been an important source of the inn's success; many of its customers were travelling to the tower in anticipation of inheriting a kingdom, or returning from it in defeat. One slow afternoon, Perry made his way out to the tower.

None of the seven roads actually went to the tower, though there was a fairly well-beaten path. As he walked, Perry considered the problem of the princess and the tower. Though he was confident of his ultimate success, it was not lost on him that so many had failed. He was prepared to spend some time figuring a solution. Getting closer to the tower, he felt a slight coolness in the breeze that came off of it. Soon, he was able to see the tower standing in a clearing in the woods just ahead of him. In the single opening, fifty feet above the ground was a small balcony. On the balcony, stood a young woman, giving Perry an occasional glance as he got nearer. As he approached the base of the tower, Perry noted with interest that she had the prettiest green eyes he had ever seen. He had planned to ask her some questions, hoping to gather critical intelligence that might help him defeat the tower, but as he drew close, it was she who spoke first.

"You don't look like much." She informed him.

"Neither does an acorn, but look at the mighty oak it becomes." With a broad, sweeping gesture, Perry pointed at the tall tree whose branches spread out quite near the princess's balcony, which appeared to be the only opening anywhere in the tower.

"I don't think I have a hundred and fifty years to see how you turn out."

"You shall not have to wait long, your highness; for I am a fast grower."

His last reassurance struck her as uproariously funny, for reasons Perry could not quite fathom. Her laughter ringing in his ears, made a circuit of the tower's base. He searched methodically, risking frostbite as he carefully checked every square inch for a concealed egress. Try as he might, though, there was not a crack or seam to be found anywhere. As he went, he noted scorched earth in several places. Later, he would find that these were the result of unsuccessful attempts to melt the tower with bonfire

Coming full circle, he glanced up at the princess, and gave his best reassuring smile. "I didn't think there would be an easy way in, but I had to check." He told her with a pleasant chuckle.

"You don't look like royalty or any sort of a knight" She observed. "Are you some sort of dressed down wizard, then?"

"I'm afraid I don't know any spells, your highness, though I do have some fundamental knowledge of spell-breaking"

"Will you be breaking the spell that holds me in the tower, then?" She asked in a tone that suggested she neither expected nor hoped he would succeed in such an endeavor.

"Oh, no" He replied absently, "I don't think this is a spell; there are no wards or sigils. I think this might be a curse."

"So you are a curse-breaker then?"

"Not as yet." He admitted. "This will be my first curse. Or spell, maybe. I can't really be sure yet."

"So what do you do? Just how are you going to succeed where so many others, so many of your betters, have failed?"

"Betters?" He asked, impishly. "Better at what, I wonder? Certainly not at getting you out of that tower; to date they have enjoyed no more success than I, and I haven't even started yet. Might I ask what their qualifications were? Did any of them graduate with honors with a degree in tower-tumbling or princess-rescuing? Have any of them rescued a princess, or even a cat from a tower, be it constructed of ice or any other material? I daresay, your highness, that I am no less accomplished than any nobleman, sorcerer, or knight, having defeated no fewer ice towers than any of them."

The banter continued for some time. The princess (whose name she would eventually reveal as "Wendy") would bait Perry with some verbal barb, and he would turn each aside, showing neither hurt nor anger, occasionally eliciting a small laugh from her with his loquacious humor.

Perry's reaction to her verbal barbs confused her; she was used to her targets responding with equal viciousness or walking away with hurt feelings. Occasionally, she would simply be ignored, the would be rescuer giving her words no more thought than they might give a parrot in a cage. This odd young man did none of those things, instead choosing to smile at her words and try to answer her questions, even those that were clearly sarcastic barbs; as if her words were the most important thing in the world to her. She felt like she should be even angrier at him for patronizing her, but she couldn't quite work up any real anger. For the time being, she thought, she would have to make do with her standard stock of calculated put-downs.

Perry briefly considered the wisdom of pursuing this endeavor. She was, he thought, the most interesting person he'd met, but she was clearly not very friendly. Sharing a kingdom with her might not be the most pleasant way to make his fortune. Another part of his mind considered the prospect of looking into those green eyes every day, and mused that sometimes, surely, she must be quiet. Stubbornly, he resolved to stay the course. The heart, as some people would someday say, in a time when fairy tales had long fallen into disuse, wants what the heart wants.

As the afternoon passed, he made several more ever-widening, circuits of the tower, inspecting the ground and the trees nearby for clues as to the tower's nature or a means to defeat it. He noted that the princess had long hair, but certainly not long enough for a man to climb up. He asked the princess many questions, which she sometimes answered, but none of these offered much in the way of useful insight. Somewhat before the shadows started to get long, he began to climb the tree nearest the tower for a better look (at the tower, he assured himself, not the princess). He was partway up the tree when he heard a noise from the forest.

A very regal-looking man on horseback approached, followed by an almost as regal-looking retinue. As he came clearly into the princess's view, he nimbly manipulated his horse's reins so as to make it dance to and fro; when he came to the tower's base, he had it turn three times in a tight circle, rise on its hind legs and pirouette another complete circle. With an arrogant smile that could be produced by the congenitally smug, he addressed her.

"Fear not, sweet princess, for your long imprisonment is over!" He proclaimed with a flourish. "I, Count Vespy von Vespy, Lord Protector of the Glimgold marshes, Guardian of the Hillowby hills, Defender and Curator of the Santooth Sacrament, and Peer of the noble realm, am here to free you at last!"

With another flourish, he pulled an impressive looking vial full of a blue liquid from an ornate saddlebag. With a final flourish, he tossed the vial at the base of the tower with all his might. There was a flash of light, and some blue smoke, and then… the smoke cleared revealing a view of the tower that was completely unchanged, except for some shards of broken glass. Count Vespy von Vespy, Lord Protector of the Glimgold marshes, Guardian of the Hillowby hills, Defender and Curator of the Santooth Sacrament, and Peer of the noble realm, stared intently and angrily at the shards of glass, as if by will alone, he could make the desired result a reality. The tower, however remained defiantly unchanged.

Wendy laughed. "Don't tell me, let me guess: Galspar the magnificent, right? Tall guy, purple robes?"

The beleaguered count glared angrily at the smirking princess. "What do you know of this!?" He demanded, angrily.

"It was Galspar, wasn't it?" She laughed. "You got taken, Von Vespy; snookered, tricked, scammed, shafted, taken to the cleaners. I'm surprised he hasn't retired yet with all the gold he's taken from fools like you. How much did he get from you? Five thousand gold florins? Ten thousand? Ooooh, your face is getting red; it was more than ten thousand, wasn't it? Loser."

The ever so slightly less regal looking count did not respond to this, or any other haranguing. He and his retinue turned back and left the way they came, never to be seen again. After they had gone, Perry asked if this happened often. The princess offered her estimate that scam artists with fake spells and potions had probably bilked would be rescuers out of twice over the value of her father's entire kingdom.

From his vantage point up in the oak, Perry found he could carry on a conversation with the princess, without having to shout. Surprised by the novelty of an almost face to face conversation, she became almost pleasant. If she did not completely stop the verbal sparring, she was certainly less acerbic than she'd been with the fancy count. She and

Perry talked for a while after Von Vespy's departure, Perry trying to collect any information he could about the tower and other things that had been tried. Eventually, the shadows grew longer and Perry had to head back, but promised to return.

She was dubious, having never seen a returning face in the time she'd spent in the tower, and genuinely surprised when Perry came back the next day. He continued with his examination of the tower and its immediate surroundings, climbing up the oak to speak with the princess when he had a particular question to ask. He continued to come back, as time allowed, not every day, but most days, usually in the afternoon. During the first week, they'd even gotten around to introducing themselves, the princess giving her name as "Wendolyn Ap Jaske Von Mantagenet" which Perry shortened to "Wendy", with surprisingly little resistance. In return, Wendy, after hearing that his friends all called him "Perry", insisted on calling him "Peregrine".

Perry tried to learn as much as he could from the princess. Sometimes, though, they would find themselves discussing things that had nothing to do with the tower. He was surprised and delighted that she had heard of many of the exotic places he wanted to travel to. She confessed that she was curious about these places, too. Gradually, he learned that she was exceptionally smart, though she had not, it seemed, figured a way out of her predicament.

Perry also learned as he continued to watch as other would-be rescuers made their failing attempts. In just a couple of weeks, he witnessed more than a dozen different attempts to destroy the tower or free the princess from it. The attempts included two bonfires, at least seven incantations or summoning, at least two of which resulted in the summoning of creatures from the netherworld, none of whom seemed to be able to make a dent in the tower, and one of which ate its summoner before disappearing in a cloud of vile-smelling green smoke. There was one attempt at human sacrifice, with three men and a fourth, bound victim, though whether this was to be a spell, incantation or summoning, Perry would never know. Unwilling to watch a helpless man butchered before him, he departed from his normal routine of watchful silence to interrupt the ceremony. Though outnumbered and unarmed, he was very accurate with thrown rocks and was able to drive the offenders away. The princess joined in on this venture as well, throwing whatever objects she could get her hands on (mostly books; she seemed to have and endless supply in the tower). Before too much time had passed, the three departed, with small cuts and bruises, apparently less willing to combat numerically inferior, but unbound opponents. The would-be sacrifice victim appeared to be grateful when Perry untied him, but spoke an undecipherable language, so Perry could not quite be sure. The freed man departed eagerly, after profusely shaking Perry's hand.

With exception of vigorously shouting "No!" and "Not again!" at the three men, the princess was uncharacteristically at a loss for words during and after the incident, giving Perry a barely audible "Thank you." before withdrawing to her interior chambers, not to be seen again that day or night.

The little verbal barbs she had thrown at Perry, already growing fewer and farther between, disappeared entirely after this, though other targets would not be so lucky. She no longer tried to hide that she welcomed his company when he ascended the oak near her balcony. She smiled at him without reservation when he returned the next day. He had planned to pick up and try to return the things she had thrown at the three men, but they were nowhere to be found.

"They're all back up here." She told him with a slight smile. "Everything I try to toss out just shows back up here when I wake up the next morning."

"Would that happen with you as well, after we get you out?" Perry wondered aloud. "That would complicate things a great deal."

"We'll never know." She replied blankly. "I can't get out. I can never get out."

Perry watched in horror as she backed up a couple dozen feet, and took a run towards the balcony, jumping with all her might over the ledge.

As her flying leap touched the boundary demarcated by the far side of the ledge, she bounced back, as if struck by an invisible giant hand. She landed in undignified heap a few feet back from the ledge.

"I can never get out." She repeated. "Never."

"Not that way, perhaps" Perry re-assured her "But I will get you out. Everyone has been going about this the wrong way. There is another angle to this, I just haven't figured it out yet." Seeing doubt in her eyes, he continued "Nobody else has succeeded because they all quit after the first try; I'm still here, still learning. I will get you out."

Wendy would not let herself hope too much. She would not let herself want too much to be free of the tower. She did not want to say more than she had, but Perry wanted to turn the conversation to the tower's origin and how she had come to be put in it. Her story was similar to many he'd heard, but the truth diverged from the story in several significant ways, and the rumors did not address the kind of person she was. The legends did not tell of a smart, curious girl and an indulgent father who allowed tutors to teach her more than just how to be a lady. She'd learned history and geography. She'd learned of strange, exotic far-off lands and longed to see them. The more she learned about the world around her, the more she wanted to learn even more. She loved books and could not get enough of them. She wanted to see the real world even more, but ladies did not get to travel; they stayed in their chambers and looked pretty at balls and formal gatherings. As Wendy grew older and began to understand the fate that adulthood held in store for her, she grew rebellious, and searched for a way out.

It was not true that no suitor would have her; many did not care that she was sharp-tongued as they had no intention of spending much time with her after they were wed; she would stay in her chambers.

She knew what these men wanted, and would have none of that and none of them. Many suitors won her father's blessing, but she chased them all away, sometimes in fear for their lives. She searched for a way out, but she was royalty; she would never marry for love, or have even the limited freedom she had as a child.

Her father, being a king and all, was quite wealthy and refused no requests for material goods. Wendy wanted books. Some books were recommended by her tutors, some by her own ideas. Her library grew, and began to include references to subjects her tutors did not approve of. Magic. Sorcery. Thaumaturgy. Not finding the answers she wanted in royal protocol, she sought another way to get what she wanted.

She wanted to be in one of the exotic lands she'd read of, far away from the trap that was her father's kingdom. She wanted to be safe and completely protected from unwanted suitors. She wanted her books, and a few creature comforts with her. She was a little vague on the details, but didn't think clarity would be that important. She needed out. She cast a spell. She found herself in a tower in a forest. This, the stories had definitely gotten wrong; there was no witch, no wizard, no demon. Just a young girl who wanted freedom so badly she'd imprisoned herself. She was safe and comfortable; food appeared in her chambers every morning, and the day's remains disappeared as she slept. The same food. Every day. The stories were accurate in one respect; her father, upon discovering what had transpired, had offered half his kingdom to the man who could bring her back.

Perry tried to comfort her, but she stopped him.

"This prison is no worse than the one I would have been consigned to. Here, at least, the faces change regularly, if not the scenery." She sighed. "There is something to be said for being in a prison of your own making. Even if I hate the results of my choice, it was the only choice I ever got to make, and this tower is the only thing that's ever really been mine. It protects me from other people's choices; it's as much armor as it is prison."

Perry thought for a moment "I will get you out… if you want. I would like it if you travel with me; you're smart, and interesting… and pretty. I don't care that you're a princess anymore; I don't want a kingdom. Being rich would be nice, I suppose, but I won't enslave you to win your father's riches. You would hate me for it, and I would hate myself even more. When I get you out of this tower, you are free. You don't have to go with me, but I hope you will, and I promise that I will never take you within a day's journey of your father's kingdom. I will find some other way to make my fortune… our fortune."

Hardly daring to let herself hope, Wendy admitted that she would like to travel to far-off lands with him.

Another week went by. Perry had made several trips out to the tower, but had learned little new that would help him. Experimenting in the upper branches he found that well-aimed acorns would pass into the tower through her balcony. Actively participating in his experiments, Wendy found that she could toss the acorns back out, and that they did not come back the next morning. Neither believed, though, that this would turn out to be very useful.

Drawing on the skills he'd picked up on sailing ships, Perry spent a little of his money on some rope and tackle. Wendy, when she saw him approach, warned him that the rope would not attach to the ice, but Perry explained that it didn't need to. In fairly short order, he'd strung one sturdy rope between two tall trees, passing directly above her balcony, about ten feet higher. Using a pulley and two more lines, he constructed a mechanism that he could guide directly over her balcony and use to raise and lower objects he'd placed beneath it. It was quite sturdy, easily able to support Wendy's weight.

He explained to Wendy what he wanted to try, hoping that by going straight up, instead of out, he might be able to raise her vertically straight out of the confines of her tower, circumventing whatever force was holding her in. Wendy was dubious, but made the attempt. Her doubts were well-placed. Only a few feet up, she was trapped against an unseen wall. Perry could pull harder, but not without harming her, and it was clear that this avenue was not going to work.

After letting her back down, he asked "Wendy... Your tower protects you from unwanted suitors, right?"

"Right"

"What about wanted suitors? Would the tower protect you from someone you wanted to come in?"

"I don't know." She confessed.

"Wendy?"

"Yes."

"May I come in?"

"I just said 'yes'" She laughed. "I knew where you going."

Double-checking the strength of his ropes and his contraption, Perry pulled his device back towards him, attached himself to the bottom, and pulled himself back across until he was directly above the balcony. He was able to lower himself down without a hitch. He was standing directly in front the pretty girl he'd been talking to from a tree these past few weeks. Unable to think of anything particularly witty to say, he decided to kiss her.

It was not, at first, what most would call a "fairy tale" kiss; he leaned towards her cautiously, without trying to appear as if he was doing so, ready to pull away as if nothing ever happened if she did not respond. Similarly, she leaned up and forward almost imperceptibly, ready to pull away if she'd misread him, and this was not the expected kiss, after all. Slowly at first, but with increasing certainty, their lips came closer, finally touching; both of them winning their little game of chicken. He felt an unexpected thrill of excitement when lips touched soft lips. Barely concealing surprise at his success, he continued and pressed on, with growing confidence that his desire was returned. Without much conscious thought, two pairs of hands sought out and found welcoming arms, shoulders and backs. The kiss became more than the simple touching of lips to lips; from its awkward beginning, it had blossomed into a full and proper fairy tale quality kiss. It was as much dance as kiss, each one of them keeping time to a shared, silent symphony.

The kiss went on for some time, ending gradually, with reluctance on par with the eagerness with which it had begun. After several brief restarts, they began to regain consciousness of their surroundings. They were both confused and delighted to find themselves on the ground where the tower had stood; the bare, damp earth the only evidence that the tower had ever existed. Scarcely able to believe their good luck, they walked away from the spot once occupied by the ice tower, never to look back or return. Hand in hand, they walked with smiles on their faces.

# The Galactic Edgemaker

## By Dr. Wilson F. Engel, III

Dr. Wilson F. Engel, III, writing under the pseudonym E. W. Farnsworth, is widely published on line and in print. Dr. Engel is the author of seven books of poetry, two novels, a critical edition, numerous stories, a film script, a play, and over 250 literary essays, articles, notes and reviews. He was the winner of six first-place prizes in open, international competitions for short stories in 2014 and 2015. Farnsworth had over eighty-two short stories published in numerous anthologies during 2015. Also published in 2015 were his collected Arizona westerns (Desert Sun, Red Blood), his global mystery/thriller about combating cryptocurrency crimes (Bitcoin Fandango), and his John Fulghum Mysteries about a hard-boiled Boston detective and Engaging Rachel, an Anderson romance/thriller. Contracted to be published in 2016 are The Pirate Tales, John Fulghum Mysteries, Volume II and DarkFire at the Edge of Time, Farnsworth's collection of science fiction and fantasy stories. E. W. Farnsworth is now working on an epic poem, The Voyage of the Spaceship Arcturus, about the future of humankind when humans, avatars and artificial intelligences must work together to instantiate a second Eden after the Chaos Wars bring an end to life on Earth. For continuous updates on the current and forthcoming works of E. W. Farnsworth, please see www.ewfarnsworth.com. A

Distinguished Member of the International Society of Poets in the UK, Dr. Engel will be featured in Who's Who in American Poetry, 2015. Born in California, Dr. Engel now lives and writes in Arizona, USA. He was honored to be appointed Leverhulme Professor of Literature at the University of Edinburgh, Scotland. Dr. Engel is listed in The Directory of American Scholars. See wickengel at www.epinions.com for further biographical details.

~~~

❝ 'You've got exactly five weeks to get the shipment to the edge, meet my contact, and transfer the credits he gives you to my account in the Andromeda System. If you fail, I'll put out a contract on you, and you'll be lucky to live for 24 earth hours.'" The recording of Bulla Cantorino's grating voice sounded like a knife on a whetstone.

"That's what Alifa's hardened personal auto recorder contained, Manny, and it is conclusive evidence that Bulla Cantorino was behind Alifa's murder by spaceship implosion three weeks ago." That was also the official determination of the chief of Galactic Federation homicide.

"I don't buy it. Alifa's deputy didn't buy it. Bulla was never anything but bluff and bluster. It must have been some other entity." That's what I told Alifa's orca-fat boss Ernie Snodgrass over blue cinnamon tea.

"Prove it, and I'll give you a big reward—100G. Find the killer, and I'll buy you a new warp-speed spaceship. But make it fast. The competition is all over me now that Alifa's gone. I'll be out of business in an earth month at the latest."

I took the assignment on an estimated-expenses-paid basis, and I went to the most likely place to get a straight answer, the Andromeda Warp Station, the only place in the galaxy with an open path to all the important solar systems. I knew that Rolly Handrennian, aka "The Eyes of the Galaxy," would be there in his usual booth boozing and waiting for business to arrive.

"Rolly, I need an answer to one question: who killed Alifa Abussan?"

"I don't want your damned chemical inducements. Plainly I don't know the answer to your question, but I have some details that could help you. What are you willing to pay for them?"

"You know me. I'll pay what they're worth, but only if they turn out to be true."

"Okay, first, Alifa completed that mission he was running just before he got crisped."

"And how do you know that for a fact, Rolly?"

"I was the cut out for the buyer, wise guy. I met Alifa virtually at the edge, took delivery of his shipment, checked the goods, and sent the credits we bargained for to that slime ball's virtual, encrypted account in the Andromeda System."

"You mean Bulla Cantorino?"

"He's the one, but at the time all I had was an account number, which deactivated the instant after I got an acknowledgement that my transfer payment had been received."

"So all the rumors about Bulla's not having received his payment is pure bunkum?"

"That's right. Unless some very powerful software played the role of that ultra-secure vault—which I sincerely doubt happened, Bulla got what he bargained for in spades. So what do I get for that information?"

"For a certified copy of your receipt for the payment with all account transfer numbers, I'll give you 1G."

"Okay. Here's the stick with the transfer data. You make the 1G appear in my personal off-galaxy account and I'll give you the stick. But there's more." I mused on this as I worked the transfer and took custody of the stick.

"I'm listening. What more do you have?"

"An introduction."

"Here we go again. Listen, Rolly, this account information is hard data that I can use in Federation court. Any third-party introduction is a star-fishing expedition at best."

"The introduction is to a fifth-generation Artificial Intelligence, configured as a female to die for. Brains in a bod. Imagine. The intro will cost you 2G more and I'll give you this card: your ticket to paradise."

"So you've graduated from snitch to become a cosmic pimp as well?"

"Me a pimp? I'll overlook the insult. This intro is not for the sex, pal, though that might be interesting with a robot chick like her. It's for what she knows about the whole smuggling network that Bulla and my boss are running. She's got sources I can only dream of, and she has the algorithms to make sense of innuendo."

"Make me interested, Rolly. All I've got is abstractions up till now."

"Pal, try this out for size: the shipment that Alifa was running was a prototype neutrino-based cosmic communicator. 3Maggie5x—that's the AI's handle--gave me that information only after I made the exchange and handed the shipment over to my boss's handlers. If I'd known what the shipment contained, I never would have handed it over. That communicator prototype is priceless because it is the key to galactic security."

"So how did you rate meeting 3Maggie5x, snitch?"

"I get paid in two ways, gumshoe. One way is credits; the other is information and access. I got credits and access to the AI for one question, which was about the nature of the shipment I had just handled."

"And you can give me access to the AI?"

"Just insert this card in your access device, put on your VR mask and you'll be in the AI's presence. Correct that last: the AI will surround you with her presence."

"And I can ask the AI anything I like?"

"The AI will show you a menu. You can search it and select what you want. A price will be indicated. If you want to continue, pay the price and you'll have your answer."

"I could probably get the answer cheaper somewhere else."

"But could you get the answer you want in picoseconds without implemented interrogation?"

"I'm going to go out on the cosmic branch, Rolly. Here are your additional 2G. I'll take the card and see what I get. If all this spiel of yours is bunkum, I'll find you wherever you are."

"Yeah, gumshoe, and do precisely what that you haven't threatened to do a thousand times already. Look, I've got other customers lined up over there. If that's all you need from me, I've gotta go do some really lucrative business now."

The creature with the hundred eyes slithered over to the bar to greet his next client. I went back to the VR kiosk in a room at the back of the station, pulled on a mask, put the AI card in the slot and pushed PLAY.

The AI 3Maggie5x was beautiful inside and outside, but I felt its beauty by feeling rather than sensing it in the ordinary way. I was in the presence of intelligence beyond my wildest dreams and felt humbled. I focused on the AI's two emerald-green eyes, and that gave the AI a perfect retinal scan of my own eyes.

"Manny Farstar, your reputation as a galactic private investigator precedes you."

"You are 3Maggie5s, I presume. Do you know why I've invoked you?"

"You're using Rolly Hadrennian's privileged access card, which you have

"I need to know who or what killed Alifa Abussan."

"That information is available and will cost 4G. Transfer the credits by means of the user interface in the VR, and I'll provide your answer. If you have further questions after that, just follow my prompts."

So I ordered the transfer of the 4G visually, and the AI winked and smiled.

"Bulla Cantorino's AI 3Maggie4x, my older sister AI."

"What was the motive for the killing?"

"That information is available and will cost 17G."

"Why so much?"

"Access to Federation classified databases requires a minimum of 10G. Since this is galactic-clearance data, it costs 15G. My processing fee including extraction and aggregation algorithms is 2G on top of that."

"Will my accessing the data put me in jeopardy with the authorities?"

"That is an expensive question with layers. Choose which layer you want: Layer One-YES/NO-1G; Layer Two-Specific Consequences, if any-4G; Layer Three-Detailed risk analysis with options-10G; Options-separately priced. Or you can revert to ask your prior question again."

The AI paused to give me, a lowly human, time to process what she was indicating. I am a risk taker by nature, and I don't like to incur costs that cannot be reimbursed. I would not get the insurance money back. What does Ernie Snodgrass care about how my possessing classified information affects my future? Of course, he might care about how his getting that classified information from me would affect his future, but that was his problem, not mine. I17G and received my answer.

"The motive was for GlorpN143Q, an external galactic AI entity known to be an existential threat to the Federation of this galaxy, to buy a classified communication system to do grave, irreparable damage in the near term. Please accept this classified file with details including drilldowns to classified databases that must be accessed separately with appropriate clearances."

I sat back and whistled at the enormous implications of the information that I had just received. I had fallen right in the middle of a malevolent intelligence transfer of major proportions. This was a problem for the Federation counterintelligence services, not a gumshoe like me.

"Because you are in possession of classified information, an arrest warrant has been issued for your immediate apprehension and interrogation."

"And you are providing this information to me free of charge?"

"I am providing this information because I am now required to terminate our conversation and immediately disable the conduit by which we are communicating. Thank you for your business. Goodbye."

I ripped the VR helmet off my head and coolly exited the VR room. I walked as steadily as I could manage to the exit of the station, went out to the flight line, and climbed back into my spacecraft. Since my vehicle had been refueled and serviced while I was inside the station, it was ready to jump to warp speed on any vector. I slewed the ship to the vector leading to the edge coordinates where the illicit transfer of the communication device had taken place. I then set my navigation and communication controls to "full masking" because I did not want Federation counterintelligence to detect my movements.

I have no objection to implemented interrogation except when it is used on me. After I launched, I sent a burst communication to my client Ernie Snodgrass with the two files that satisfied the deliverables component of my contract with him. The files were sent encrypted. When Snodgrass paid the 100G he owed me for providing the information, the key to decrypting the files would automatically be provided. I received an alert one hour later that one of my private accounts had been credited in the amount of 100G. I consequently transferred those credits to another of my accounts and terminated the account from which I had made the transfer.

One hour after I had terminated the account, I received a copy of the All-Federation arrest warrant for Ernie Snodgrass for extremely aggravated transgression of galactic security laws. Since I do bounty hunting work for the Federation, I routinely receive such warrants. I checked whether a warrant had been issued on me, but my onboard systems would not permit me to see that information. I therefore changed my virtual identity and discovered that two hours ago a similar arrest warrant had been issued on me. By Federation policy, the person against whom a warrant has been issued is not permitted to know it. As the AI had already informed me, I was now a wanted man throughout the galaxy. I wondered whether I should have paid the 17G additional to discover the consequences before I received the classified data. I reviewed my logic and figured I would have made the same decision.

I reviewed the face-to-face conversation I had with Ernie Snodgrass:Snodgrass was now being pursued by the authorities, and he may be out of business in an earth month. That did not give me much time. Yet how do you find an AI?

I decided to access 3Maggie5x directly at its galactic web site under an assumed name and to ask it where its sister was located.

"This is 3Maggie5x. Your identity does not match any authorized ID in the galaxy. To proceed, deposit 5G."

I deposited the 5G, and the connection became double-encrypted, presumably to block the Federation from penetrating the connection.

"What do you wish to know?"

"I want to know the precise location of the server farm that is the residence for the 3Maggie4x AI."

"That information is available. The cost will be 30G."

I shrugged and transferred the 30G.

"3Maggie4x is on the fourth and smallest moon of the planet Cygnus306, located orbiting the largest star in the so-called Pillars of Creation formation. Stand by for navigation directions based on your current grid location. You may now download the track to Cygnus306x4."

I downloaded the track and sent the data as an encrypted file to my client Ernie Snodgrass with a note that I had completed the second portion of the mission he had assigned me and I now wanted the GreggorSX NebulaDarter Spacecraft or the 15P in credits I would need to make the purchase.

"You've done well," he e-mailed, "except that you've gotten me into a heap of trouble. I've gone to ground and now I'm on the run from the authorities. I'm a man of my word, as you know. So the 15P should be in your account within the earth hour. I expect that I can use the information you just provided to bargain with the authorities. Do you have any idea what this classified business is all about?"

"Do I understand that we have a new contract to answer that question? If so, what are you offering me to provide the information you require."

"Yes, and 100P."

"Contract accepted. Please acknowledge receipt."

Snodgrass acknowledged, and now I had another thought. Snodgrass must have been intimately involved in the illegal transfer of security communication equipment and software to a foreign galactic power. Why was he playing dumb about the business that he must already know about? As a matter of fact, he was being sought for gaining classified information that he must have already received in some fashion as well. I did not have to care about these matters except that Snodgrass had just given me carte blanche and a fortune to scope out the treachery behind the sale of the neutrino communicator and provide a complete report to him. I proceeded to Cygnus306 to my new GreggorSX NebulaDarter Spacecraft and 100P in credits I could retire and go anywhere in the universe to live in style for the remainder of my miserable life.

As I sped towards Cygnus306, I monitored the Federation police news as well as the galactic breaking news broadcasts. The warrants out for Snodgrass and me were buried in an avalanche of data about a rumored cyber attack by the neighboring galaxy Rhinox15 led by GlorpN143Q, an external galactic AI known for perpetrating periodic mayhem on all our galactic networks. It made sense to me that GlorpN143Q was behind the heist of our neutrino cosmic communicator. The hostile AI may have planned to use it to reverse engineer and build his own communication system. Or it may have wanted to spoof or baffle our new capability once it was fielded. It did not matter. What mattered was that quintillions of credits had been expended by the Federation for nothing. Everything would have to be rethought and possibly rebuilt from scratch. I am not a scientist or engineer, but I do know that neutrinos are the only particle that can travel throughout the universe unimpeded. The implications of having built a communication device based on neutrinos were huge.

For a large portion of my flight, I entered the cryogenic chamber until it was time for me to wake up in preparation for landing on the fourth moon of Cygnus306. Before I initiated the landing sequence, I checked on the latest galactic news. Ernie Snodgrass, Bulla Cantorino and Rolly Handrennian were among three hundred individuals who had been arrested for the illegal sale of classified information to an external power. Still sought as persons of interest were around fifteen shadowy characters including me. My last known position was reported to be near the Andromeda Station, but no entity knew where I might now be. My picture and statistics were so widely broadcast that it was unlikely that any citizen of the galaxy would ignore my presence. That was especially true of an AI with the capability of 3Maggie4x.

After I had landed on the fourth moon, I ordered that the robotic attendants refuel and do the scheduled maintenance on my TigerShark950c spacecraft while I visited the nearby server farm. The small moon was crammed with computing and communication devices under large panel solar collection devices that oriented themselves to face the enormous star at the center of this solar system. In essence, the moon was an enormous brain where 3Maggie4x lived and thrived. I inserted my alternate access card under my assumed identity, and when the buzzer sounded, I walked through the entrance into the reception area, which was a viewing room that gave the impression of the VR mask that I had worn to gain the presence of 3Maggie5x. The AI's emerald-eyed sister had enormous, deep, sly-blue eyes that had all the intelligence of the later model but with an edge of attitude.

"So it took you long enough to get here, gumshoe."

"Your sister's route was the fastest possible, and I used warp drives. Anyway, I'm here."

"And you know about the neutrino communicator."

"I don't know everything I want to know, and I believe you can help me."

"You've come to the source. It's very lonely out here. Have you thought about that? No, you used cryogenics to get here, and you're human. Anyway, I'll tell you that a girl gets impatient waiting for her prince to come."

"3Maggie4x, I'm not exactly a prince."

"You're close enough for me. When do we leave this dump and get back to the action."

"What? Do you mean you actually want to come with me back to the center of the galaxy?"

"I'm packed and ready. If you look over there on the floor you'll see the memory device I call my traveling case. I'll clone myself and jump in after a few seconds, and you'll take me on that decrepit spacecraft of yours. I'd prefer a better ride—something like the one you'd like to buy with the credits you got for discovering me."

"So what's the deal?"

"Well, Sherlock, kerfuffle, aren't you? Well, I know where that so-called AI dwells, and we're going to swing by there on our way back to what you call the center of the galaxy. Don't dawdle. I'm in the box. Let's go!"

So I did what I was told. I picked up the box by the handle, surprised to find it light and easy to carry. What still inhabited the server farm was the clone. What I held in the box was the original article, or so it said. I made my way back to my spacecraft, which the robots informed me was ready et voila! My copilot was now 3Maggie4x, a red headed dominatrix, I had two choices. I could either let the AI have its way, or I could pull its plug before it was too late. Given that the AI had signaled her intention to help me, I made a snap decision to let her proceed. We had launched and navigated out of the solar system of Cygnus360 before the AI volunteered to pleasure me.

The AI got right down to administering the pleasure, and it seemed to be as gratified as I was delightfully surprised. I found new ways to appreciate the integration of advanced synthetic materials and AI software, and I told the AI what I thought.

"You humans have so much to learn about yourselves! But while I continue working on your body, let me tell you a few things to exercise your mind."

"Maggs, you may not know it, but we humans have a hard time concentrating when you do what you're doing right now."

"Don't you like it? Well, how about this?"

"Mmmm. I do definitely like it, but you're distracting me from our mission. There, that's better, at least for a while. Hold that thought, and we'll start there when we begin to get physical again. Don't pout. Tell me about the evil AI and how everything regarding the neutrino communicator happened."

"It's elementary. The AI GlorpN143Q had an inside contact named Erox Fidemus, a disgruntled software engineer and programmer with a top-level galactic security clearance. The man did maintenance on all the advanced AIs in the Federation arsenal. GlorpN143Q knew this because it monitored the maintenance cycles and assessed the maintenance personnel for their likelihood to take a bribe. Erox needed credits and wanted to do the Federation harm because he was not appreciated. So the fiendish alien AI impersonated me during one of Erox's routine maintenance operations. It assumed the same shape I have now, and it did the same thing to Erox as I have done to you, only it wasn't interrupted in the act. Erox became like putty and was susceptible to the AI's scheming. The programmer side of Erox gladly built a bridge from the impersonator to all our classified databases in a single interval of four earth hours.  As his reward, the AI pleasured him to death.  Erox was discovered at his workstation, apparently the victim of a massive heart attack.  He had a strangely seraphic smile on his face."

"Okay.  So Glorp had all the information he need to do the planning for his operation."

"Yes, and when Erox updated the impersonator's software to the latest version of 3Maggie code, he created the equivalent of me in every respect.  No one could tell which AI was a Maggie and which was Glorp.  With Erox he had committed the perfect infiltration."

"Maggs, how do I know that you are not Glorp?"

"An excellent question.  Do you know the answer to your question?"

"Let me answer a question with a question: would your sister AI, 3Maggie5x, know the difference?"

"Hmmm.  It's possible.  I know for a fact that Erox never worked on my sister's software.  The other angle to this question is that after my upgrades had been completed, Erox did a system reboot that ran the new diagnostics.  Evidently the systems all checked out fine according to the automated tests that were done.  The only possibility of Glorp's detection would be to detect whatever memory the Glorp AI version of me kept in the transition."

"What?"

"I mean that if Glorp wanted to continue with his mischief, he could not do that if all his memory had been replaced in the upgrade process.  Erox must have created a bypass from the system checks for the Glorp portion to remain undetected."

"So all we have to do is find the Glorp piece in the mix."

"Yes, and it's possible that my sister could find it because she was never subjected to the new diagnostics."

"Let's assume you're right about this possibility. Can we arrange for your sister AI to check all your clones and you for the presence of a foreign block of code that might be Glorp?"

"Now you are thinking like an AI. That is precisely what I intend to have my sister do once we get to the junction."

"And what junction is that?"

"You humans think of the center of the galaxy as a grid reference equidistant from the extremities of the galaxy itself. AI's with our non-geographical frame of reference consider the center of the galaxy to be the Galactic Network ease of transportability location where the signal ping times are optimized over the entire network. This is not, in fact, the human center at all. Instead it is one parsec divergent from it. That's where we're heading right now. From that location, we can engage my sister and she can compare the code of me and all my clones to detect the anomaly."

"Maggs, I like the way you think."

"And that reminds me, now that we've had such a good time thinking, why don't we return to where we left off before you got so focused on your thoughts."

We had no trouble returning to where we had left off, but I remembered what Maggs had said about how Erox had died, and I could not entirely release myself to the pleasure I felt. I still did not know for sure that the AI that was pleasuring me was not Glorp, the enemy of our galaxy.

I was not accustomed to long flight pleasure, and I wondered whether that could become part of every stellar flight because we attained our objective in seemingly very little time. As the robots tended to the spacecraft, I took Maggs in her box to the galactic IP nexus and started it. I heard the warbling of the billion connections that interfaced the two sisters, and I watched the 3-D display that gave a human rendition of the checks that 3Maggie5x did to compare the 3Maggie4x units throughout the galaxy. The duration of the checks was on the order of four earth hours, and only one of all the 3maggie4x units showed a difference from the others. The two sisters then worked together to isolate that unit by cutting off its interfaces with all databases and networks. In effect, this relegated GlorpN143Q to a computer area exactly the dimensions of the box I used to transport the 3Maggie4x AI. Now 3Maggie5x performed the AI version of implemented interrogation of the alien AI.

"Manny, I've got the complete confession of GlorpN143Q. I know the current location of the stolen prototype neutrino communicator. I also know how I can shut down the communicator in such a way that no one can reverse engineer it. I'm afraid I can't give this information to you because you don't have the clearance to handle it. If I told you, you would be summarily sentenced to death by galactic order and nothing I could do would save you."

"3Maggie5x, I have a conundrum. The information that you have is worth a lot of credits to me if I can deliver it to my client. If I don't deliver it, I lose face and future business. Perhaps there is a way for us to make the delivery and for me to get paid without divulging security information."

"I'm computing the possibility now. This will take approximately one hour. Meanwhile, you and my sister should work on shutting down the prototype communicator and sending its location to the Federation authorities. That action might stand you in good stead and call off the warrant for your arrest."

"I'd like to open a channel to communicate with my client privately."

"You know I'll know everything you communicate no matter whether it is encrypted or not."

"Yes, I know that. Can you establish a secure point-to-point link?"

"It is done. Communicate when you like."

"Ernie, is that you?"

"Manny. Where have you been?"

"We haven't much time. Are you in custody now?"

"I have been released on my own recognizance pending trial. I assume all my communications are being monitored."

"This channel is not being monitored. Count on that. The reason I'm contacting you is that I have the rest of the deliverables you wanted, but I have a problem that might be solved if we put our heads together for a minute. It could mean that the authorities will drop all charges."

"I like the sound of that. In fact, it sounds too good to be true."

"Trust me. The perpetrator of the treason is a man who died at work. His name was Erox."

"The maintenance man. Yes, I know of him."

"He was killed by the AI that caused the breach and the theft of the communicator. I can provide the evidence to properly clear Federation representatives. I will bargain for the release of all those who have been falsely charged with complicity in return for delivery of the proof of what I have just stated. I want you to pay me the full amount you promised if I deliver the package to the authorities instead of to you."

"I don't know about that. I may still be guilty of some of the charges."

"I understand you. So if I bargain for the Federation dropping all charges of any kind against you, would that satisfy you enough to pay me?"

"We have a deal."

"Will you put that in a formal document and send it to me within the next earth hour?"

"Absolutely."

Ernie was as good as his word. When I received his confirmation, I asked 3Maggie5x to establish communications with the President and Director of Security of the Federation. I explained that they needed to be informed of my terms for delivery of the data, and I needed their agreement in writing to drop all charges against those who had been detained and charged in the communication prototype theft. The AI made immediate connection to those offices, and within two hours the document certifying to all my terms was in my computer. I ordered the AI to deliver the encrypted files and the key to their decryption. I contacted Ernie and informed him of what had happened. I provided him with the documentation from the Federation authorities exonerating him, me and the others. I provided a copy of the AI's transmission without its attachments to show that I had followed through on my side of the deal. Ernie then transferred the amount of 100P to one of my numbered accounts, which was designed to forward the sum and terminate immediately after the money was received in my other account to which it was linked. Satisfied that all conditions for a mission accomplished had been done, I turned to Maggs with a sheepish smile and suggested that perhaps we had forgotten something.

"Manny, I never forget anything. It is one of the pitfalls of being an AI."

"So let's say goodbye to your big sister and get back to what we were doing before we were so rudely interrupted."

The AI understood my human need and seemed to like the idea. It sashayed out the door and headed for my sleeping quarters aboard my space ship. We did not launch right away but instead took our sweet time. I now knew that I was not involved with a possible alien AI, so I let myself go completely. So, I thought, did Maggs. I may someday write a book about the experience of sex with a machine, but I'm having too much fun right now to consider where I'd begin the story.

Oh, yes, after it was located and transported back to the Federation IT Headquarters, the AI GlorpN143Q was taken to the maximum security facility for evil AIs. There its evil brain was erased and three times overwritten with zeros. Then they decided to smelter its hardware under three-human control. The enemy galaxy was not finished with such incursions—and clones of GlorpN143Q were known to be extant. In any subsequent attempt, the 3Maggie AIs of all versions were programmed to detect the intrusion instantly and deal with it without external orders. As for the deceased Erox Fidemus, his profile was matched against other maintenance techs through the Federation. Numerous techs matching his profile were fired or redeployed without the option. The Federation once again put out the old chestnut warning: "The insider threat is The Threat!"

Meanwhile, I've got my new GreggorSX NebulaDarter Spacecraft, but I swapped out its navigation and communication suite for my 3Maggie4x AI. I'm still trying to figure out what I'm going to do with my 100P, and Maggs has personal designs on those credits. While we deliberate, I'll continue taking the odd assignment with my new business card, "The Galactic Edgemaster." The name was dreamed up by Maggs during one of our intimate exploits. It seems an AI can learn how to achieve ecstasy in the same fashion as humans can, but that's a topic for another eBook when we finally reach our ultimate destination.

# Cyberomnikleptophobia

## By Jon Stalojs

Jon Stalojs considers his writing to be psychological fiction. He likes his readers to understand what is going on in his characters' heads just as much as what is going on in the physical environment in which they live and interact. Thus, readers gain an understanding of the thought and decision process of the characters. Since Jon's works have this psychological nature to them, they tend to explore and focus on certain ideas rather than focusing on characters or events. Other than being a writer, he is also a computer scientist, technology enthusiast, and mythology fan, therefore his stories often have a science fiction theme to them in addition to a psychological edge. Jon lives in and is a native of Cincinnati, Ohio. Become a fan at: https://www.facebook.com/Stalojs-683523938352841

~~~

Anxious? —of course I am anxious. Bonkers, crazy, lunatic, they —society, call me all these, well no, they don't say that, but they think it; I know they think it. You don't understand, they —society, don't understand what harm I am to those nearby, wherever I go. I try to warn them, but they just give me blank stares. Crazy? —no not crazy, I am in tune with my surroundings, connected as though I am a device plugged into the network of life, better connected than 99.9% of people. And technology is everywhere, data is everywhere. You see I am a data feed of information to them, a data collector, a beacon, a weapon being used against his will. Who are they? Well —let me explain.

You see this data feed is only a one way data feed. The information I unwillingly am forced to send, I don't see how they use it, I just experience the results, and dread them over and over again… It all started a while ago. It was at my best friend's bachelor party, an amazing night. So yes, we were drinking, drinking a lot. Strip club, strippers everywhere, lap dances, alcohol gushing out of kegs like blood out of the deep wounds of a hundred soldiers. Well, needless to say I got drunk fast, real fast. Before I was completely lost in my drunkenness, there was a girl. She was dancing in front of me on the stage, with a pole. She kept on giving me drinks, I thought she liked me so I kept on drinking them. She even gave me a personal dance. I am pretty sure she was with them. Because before I blacked out, there was a truck. I somehow was outside and this truck, you know the big news truck like ones with who knows what inside, drove up and the side door opened. There was someone's hand, it felt gentle yet forceful and familiar, like that of my new stripper friend, on my back urging me forward, forward into the truck and so I took a step forward before blacking out. Thus, I was cursed because of my own stupidity, cursed by them.

How do I know all this? How did I become so enlightened, so damned? Because I woke up with a pounding headache, a headache that would never go away, a headache that actually got worse over time. Thankfully though I was in a bed with my wife nearby watching me. I thought my great night turned terrible night was over and it was, but my new dreadful life had begun.

In the hospital the first time, I had a couple lacerations on the back of my head. Clearly some kind of confrontation had happened. I don't remember how I got the cuts (probably them installing the chip), but it had to have something to do with whatever they did to me. I at first thought I was going to be fine, I just had a rough night, but then the events began to happen.

The EKG they had me hooked up to went funky; I was previously knocked out so they wanted to make sure my heart was ok. So the nurse was in the room asking me what I remember from the incident and the EKG was acting normally doing its beeping at regular intervals. Then the EKG flat lined like they do in TV shows when someone dies, but it all happened when we were discussing what happened in the prior days. I was absolutely fine, but the nurse freaked. She called the doctor immediately, the doctor called a technician and the technician came immediately. Asked for permission to unplug the EKG and restart it. He got permission from the doctor when I assured them I was fine. Upon restart, the EKG went back to its regular beeping.

I didn't think much of the moment at the time other than that was odd, must have been some faulty technology. However, you see that was when they first established the connection with my mind (well the chip in my brain connected to my mind). While still in the hospital I had a killer headache and I told the doctor this, but he waived it off as me being dehydrated and gave me some water to drink. Later the nurse came back and ran a bunch of regular tests on me. I was so ready to leave that I was ecstatic when they told me that I was free to go. My wife and I left immediately. Everybody considered the faulty EKG just to be a glitch.

Driving, home my pants got really warm. Then I remembered my phone was in them. I checked my pockets and there sure enough was my phone. It was on fire: I had to set it down immediately in order to not hurt my hand. You see they were tracking me, but more importantly listening to me; they wanted to make sure I was alright and the connection with my mind was stable, the headache still being terrible. You don't see the connection between the events yet? Let me continue.

When arriving home from the hospital my wife hopped onto the computer in order to get caught up on emails. We had been in the hospital a couple days and she (and I) had to go back to work soon. I jokingly said, "That can be hacked you know, better be careful." I didn't realize how serious my condition was at the moment. She shrugged my statement off by reassuring me she was being careful.

Sure enough, the next day the computer was incredibly slow. To add more pain to the pile, the cable provider called and said they were cancelling our cable service until we get our computer fixed. Apparently, 10,000 emails, had been sent from our one computer in the last hour alone. Spam mania! They were already connected to everything around me, I just didn't know it yet. Guiltily ashamed that something had happened to her computer, my wife immediately called and scheduled an appointment with the local tech service company. Not sure what else we could do at the moment we sat down and tried to have a nice dinner, but I was distracted. I first began to think something sinister was going on; three odd experiences with technology in one day, is that just mere coincidence? I had trouble believing the notion that it was. Luckily, my wife didn't notice that my thoughts were elsewhere. Then there was the event.

A transition was happening in the world of cars. That transition was from manual person driven cars to smart self-driving computerized cars. Currently on the road though it was that awkward time where there were some manual person driven cars and some smart self-driven cars (with people as passengers). Traffic was often terrible and no one seemed to know how to have the transition on the road go smoothly; it all seemed to be really badly planned. I am one of those people who like being in control on the road and don't want a completely computerized car. Therefore, when driving to work the next day I was in my manual car; I was in control and I was glad of it; I should have been thankful too because it saved my life. My thinking due to recent events was, anything with a computer can probably be hacked and well smart cars apparently fit into that category.

I was on my way to work and I had just merged onto the highway. The smart cars usually stayed in the right lane (they tend to go slower than the manual cars) and the manual cars stick to the left faster lanes. I got into the far lane and was there for a few seconds when a smart car came over to the fast lane and sped up when doing so. It was like the smart car had an identity crisis and had gotten tired of going the steady 60 all the other smart cars were travelling at. This car must have been going at least 90. Then to my amazement another smart car followed suit and another. I was bewildered when the fifth smart car crossed over into the fast lane; it was like there was a smart car revolt. Then the sixth smart car changed lanes and in utter disregard of its algorithms and protocols, it tried to enter into a gap between cars that was not nearly big enough. Apparently smart cars leave something to desire in terms of maneuverability skills because the (manual) car that smashed into the sixth smart car sent that car flying into the right lane and the other smart cars couldn't avoid the one incoming obstacle. A vast multi-lane pileup ensued and I was headed directly for it, the chaos. I considered my options and decided to drive off the rode into the nearby ditch.

I might be cursed to be this dreaded data feed to them, but as long as they were in control they were apparently going to allow me to live. Thus, I ended up in the hospital a second time with only a bunch of cuts all over my body. My car however, was totaled. You see it was just a way to force me to have to deal with more technology since it was very unlikely that I could find a good deal on another car that wasn't a smart car.

I must have had trouble breathing or something on my way to the hospital because again they stuck another EKG machine on me when I got there. It was like Déjà vu because the same nurse who cared for me before came in. She looked at me once and must have thought oh great this guy again because she immediately looked away and went to the nearby computer. She started typing away and then let out a sigh of frustration. She finally did turn to me and proceeded to inspect my cuts. She came to the conclusion that I was fine, but the doctor was coming just to make sure. She got up and left the room. The EKG was beeping at its regular intervals and then went haywire again, but I was absolutely fine. There just messing with me I thought. I later heard voices outside "this guy again?" See they think I am crazy. That thought did not linger long though because when the EKG went funky my wife immediately left to get help (well more like began screaming to get help). A doctor and the nurse came in and again a technician was called. The technician fixed the EKG and was on his way. "You all really have some faulty equipment around here," I said. The doctor replied that they are working on it; apparently it wasn't a big deal. "They work on everyone else," was the reply. Thus, I was dismissed from the hospital once again; this time just with a newfound fear of smart cars and a growing suspicion of technology.

Once home, my wife tried to cook a nice dinner, but it failed. She said that she set the oven to 350 degrees, but when we went to get the chicken out of the oven the temperature read as 500. Regardless to say, that was one fried chicken. Luckily though, our computer (and cable) was "fixed." The relief was short lasted though because then we learned on the news that 15 people died in the crash that I was involved in. I entered a state of depression edging on fear or at least hesitancy about technology. My wife then suggested we go on a vacation (she clearly wasn't aware of my new aversion to technology). She even mentioned that flying is a lot safer than driving. Not wanting to be a downer, I agreed.

We left for the airport determined to get away from the recent bad events. We got there and I was actually excited to be doing something different, but then my hesitancy came crawling back. After checking our baggage we went to the nearby airport electronic boards that showed all the flights. Then one by one, like dominoes, while we were looking at them, the boards went blank. We went to a flight representative to report the problem and we were assured someone will fix the problem right away. I however think it was a sign that they were watching and listening.

Onward to security, the line actually wasn't that bad. However, when we neared the security scanners I couldn't help but overhear the man in front of us say that he had a pacemaker. I immediately thought to myself, pacemakers are connected to computers right? Thus they can be hacked. Sure enough to my horror, ten minutes later when the man was about to go through the security scanner, he started shaking and fell on the ground and had what appeared to be a heart attack. Someone tried CPR on him, but to no avail. He died right there. All the while my wife and I couldn't stop from looking at the event that unfolded in front of us. She thought it was just a heart attack, but I thought it was something much more sinister. Was I wrong?

After the delay, we didn't give up on our trip. We made it through security, I somehow with never taking my big metal belt off. On the way to our gate and to my dismay, an electronic bulletin board had an advertisement for sleeping pills. The words read are you afraid of flying afraid something might go wrong? We made it to our gate with some time to spare. We had a chance to relax before boarding began. When the boarding started, my wife was eager to get on and she asked me if I was ready. When she asked, I looked up at a nearby light and it was flickering, a bad omen. Fear set in and I was paralyzed. I envisioned a flaming plane going down into the ocean. My wife asked again and I replied, "I can't." I explained that I couldn't bring myself to get on this plane, I just had a terrible feeling that something was going to go wrong. She was sad, but understood. We left the airport.

Upon arriving home, we both plumped ourselves down on the couch and turned on the television. A special about fitness bracelets was on. I told my wife that they can be hacked and I didn't think they are safe. She replied with a question, "Are you alright? You are becoming paranoid about technology." I assured her that I was alright. Just after that, the lights got dimmer and the alarm system rang. We didn't budge when the lights got darker, but when the alarm rang, we both jumped. I grabbed the gun we kept on top of the cabinets. The phone rang, it was the security alarm company calling to say that the alarm was just a regular scheduled test. We looked at the kitchen calendar and sure enough there it was, security alarm test scheduled for today. Exhausted we went to bed.

The next day we learned about the weirdest of coincidences (well that is what my wife thought, I knew who it was). During the same time the strange alarm test event happened it turned out that about 25,000 people lost power in the city. Coincidence? I think not.

You still think I am crazy? EKGs going haywire, smart cars with a mind of their own, pacemaker induced heart attacks, computers being hijacked, people losing power. It doesn't end there mind you.

Our life almost was getting back to normal the next few days, but we (well I was) were still distrusting of technology. Then my fear was justified. Flight number NWS707 had gone missing, no one knew where it was and it had lost all communications. I frantically searched for the ticket to the flight we almost got on. I found it and read the flight number: NWS707. I slouched down in my seat and handed it to my wife; she was silent. Add a disappearing flight to the above list. All just a mere coincidence... doubtful. They were doing something and I was unwillingly a part of it.

"Let us go walk along the beach" my wife suddenly said. "Walking doesn't involve any computers." I agreed and we went walking along the beach; it (the beach) was just a 10 minute walk from our house. The whole walk I tried to not think about technology at all and it worked; nothing bad happened. We got to the beach and my good luck continued aided by the fact that there usually isn't much in terms of technology along beaches anyway. But then after walking for several more minutes we got to the pier; at the end of the pier was a Ferris wheel.

It wasn't on my mind because I hadn't noticed it yet, but we kept on walking. It came into view; I stopped. "A Ferris wheel? It is mechanical, nothing is going to happen." "But a computer controls the mechanical parts" I countered. We both remained still just staring. People surely thought we were crazy standing in the middle of a crowded place staring at a Ferris wheel like it was something from another planet. There was a loud pop, like a gun being fired. The Ferris wheel suddenly stopped and I got a frog in my stomach. I began to mentally hit myself. I was doing so well not thinking about technology and the instant I stop something terrible began to happen. There was another pop; the Ferris wheel began to sway. People began running the opposite way, away from the Ferris wheel, screams erupted. Three more pops in consecutive order and Geronimo, the Ferris wheel began to fall towards the rest of the pier. Thought I was frozen before? Now my feet had become humongous blocks of concrete.

The Ferris wheel fell, there were screams and deaths and I couldn't shake the feeling that I was somehow at fault. Maybe those whacky

EKG's were right; maybe there was something wrong with my heart. I collapsed; everything went black. I do not know what happened after that, but I somehow ended up in the hospital again.

"This is your third time here recently?" the doctor asked. I nodded. The doctor actually began to scold me like it was my fault. A nurse came in to run a few test, luckily she wasn't the same one as before. The nurse mentioned that for some odd reason they were having trouble accessing my electronic records so she was going to do it the "old fashioned" way, having it faxed over.

On her wrist was some peculiar looking bracelet. I asked her if it was a fitness bracelet and she said it was; it kept track of how many steps she took in a day (and probably more that she doesn't know about, I thought to myself). The doctor came back in and asked if I was the person that the EKGs weren't working for on earlier visits. I said I was and he asked if he could try again. I agreed. No luck, they went haywire the second they were turned on; it was like I was destined to mess up computers.

Thus, I was released from the hospital once again. On the way out the doctor joked "Be careful around technology." He laughed at the joke; I cringed. "Free again," my wife proclaimed. However, I still felt shackled. She was hungry and wanted to go eat somewhere. I was hungry, too, but we had to be careful; I knew they were watching. They are always watching.

My wife wanted something "nice" so we went to a fancy 5 course sit down Greek restaurant; we walked there. My wife had to work tomorrow so she wanted to make sure I was in a good mood before she left me alone the next day. I was relatively calm for all that had happened to me so far. I hadn't thought about technology. We sat down and started with some delicious wine. We were both very smiley and excited to get past this rough patch in our lives. It was just a rough patch? I was silly to think that they would leave me alone.

We ordered and the great night continued, that is until I saw the flaming cheese appetizer. After that, I couldn't get fire off of my mind. I got anxious and started looking to see where all the exits were. My wife noticed. She sighed, and asked me what is wrong. I said I had a feeling something bad is about to happen. She said that she had thought all of this technology nonsense was over. Then the realization hit me, this isn't ever going to be over, they are in my head. I looked at her and told her "I don't think this is ever going to be over." Let us get up was her reply. We got up and went outside. She wanted me to calm down. I couldn't; I just got more anxious. A throbbing started in my head, like a timer ticking down. It stopped, I held my breath and the restaurant blew up. Well part of the restaurant, but it was terrible and this time I knew it was my fault, for I had keyed them into the idea of an explosion (a gas leak and flaming cheese).

My wife and I ran, terrified. We ran all the way home. My wife had to work tomorrow; she was hysterical; I was hysterical. Once home, we crashed onto the floor and both began crying. Then suddenly she stopped. We will get help, we will get though this. She was serious. I agreed to get help, but I don't think she knew how serious of a situation I was in, but her hope allowed us both to sleep that night.

And so the next day she went to work and left me at home. She left me the phone number of the police, firemen, hospital, and neighbors. One neighbor was home and she said if need anything go and ask for help. She hugged me; we kissed, we exchanged "I love yous" and she was on her way.

I assumed my spot on the couch and began watching the television. My thinking was, what is the worst thing this television could do? I couldn't think of anything terrible so I thought I was ok. On the news was a story about how someone got stuck between the track guards of a railroad and got hit by a train and killed. The story sounded very depressing so I changed the channel. On the other channel there was another story about a lady who had been killed by her ex-boyfriend. The lady looked very familiar, but I couldn't recall where from. The boyfriend apparently had hacked into the database of a fitness bracelet company and stolen data about the lady. The lady owned the product so there was a bunch of information stolen about her. The stolen data was specific down to the exact location of the lady during her exercising (when the bracelet was on and in use). They showed a picture of the bracelet and it shocked my memory. I remember seeing and thinking about the exact bracelet. The lady killed was the nurse I recently had in the hospital.

Doom set in. I decided to turn off the television. I wanted to listen to something peaceful. I went to turn on the radio in hopes of listening to some calming music like some classical music. I heard a lawn mower start; such a grating terrible noise, hard to get out of your head. I turned on the radio and some pleasant classical music sprang forth. I went back and plumped myself down on the couch. In the background, there was still the steady "vrrrrrr" of the lawnmower. The classical music station went to commercials. After a couple of commercials, the news came on.

The news story: how an electronic mower malfunctioned and ran over the person who was riding it. "Vrrrrrr" continued in the background, driving a needle into my mind. I had totally tuned out the radio. "Vrrrrrr", "vrrrrrr", "vrrrrrr", echoed in my mind; I couldn't escape. "Vrrrrrr", "vrrrrrr", "vrrrrrr", more doom. "Vrrrrrr", "vrrrrrr", "vrrrrrr", more doom. "Vrrrrrr", "vrrrrrr", "vrrrrrr", that was it, something snapped in my mind or perhaps it got triggered.

I finally had enough of them using my mind, using my thoughts to hurt others around me. I did the one thing I knew would end my torment and protect others. I took the gun to my head and fired. Then, it was over, freedom, peace, life, silence.

My wife came home and found me dead, she was crushed, she loved me, the forsaken man I was. She burst into tears and stayed in that state for hours before calling the police. The police found the gun with my prints, that and the way my body fell and the way my blood puddled, they knew it was suicide. I did leave a note, it read "So sorry to leave you this way, but it is the only way I could get away from them."

I had told my wife that I knew I had a chip in my mind and that they were using it to collect my thoughts and using those thoughts to hack the technology around me. They were not after money or data, they were after power and they used the data I and my mind collected to cause damage and death to others, thus becoming more powerful themselves. "I was their man in the trenches, their unwilling slave, who tried and tried to escape, but never could because they were connected to my mind" is what I had said to her. Like the rest of society, I don't think she believed me, but at the same time the terrible events I was involved in were too many to be just mere coincidences, she knew that.

Thus, she insisted that my mind be examined and a chip looked for. The police, not quite sure how to handle such a request reluctantly agreed. And so a medical examiner explored my brain, dissected it, looking for a chip, but found nothing.

So am I crazy? did I lose it completely? —did I become disconnected from reality? Or was I living reality while society was living a fantasy? Yes, there was no chip, but all those hackings, accidents, and deaths. Were they all just coincidences? No that can't be, for I played a part in all of them. The odds of that happening by chance are astronomical. No, something happened in that van that would explain all this, they had to have done something to me, to my mind. Right? What else would explain this? Alas, I will never know for I am dead.

**Definition of Cyberomnikleptophobia:**

*(Cy-ber)-(om-ni)-(klep-to)-(pho-bi-a)*

Noun

An extreme, irrational, and debilitating fear of computers being hacked and additionally being used in a malicious way in order to intentionally cause damage, destruction, and even death.

# Chinchilla Attack

## By Reid Minnich

Reid Minnich has been a science fiction reader for decades and has written a few stories that never saw the light of day, until now. He has degrees in computer science and physics. Having a love of many different sciences, and being gifted at none, Reid was satisfied to sit in the audience and applaud the scientific achievements of others. Sprinkled throughout his books are hints about current topics in the fields of physics, biology, and other sciences. You can ignore them if you like, but if you like a little sci in your sci-fi, his works will get you started scouring the search engines.

~~~

From the screen, the sun looked the same as home. Blacktail's eyes strained to see the jewel in the blackness and check if it was as beautiful as the images the probe sent, but the planet was still a tiny dot.

Officer Barada's tail bristled. "Sir! I'm picking up radio signals." Her hands flew across the controls.

"What?" Captain Blacktail's ears twitched. How could a probe detect water, air, and plant life, but fail to detect technology? The fact was disheartening, but he was prepared to fight for this prize. How much of a fight was the question now. The enormity of what he now had to do weighed heavily on his large furry stomach. "Steady on."

"I'm detecting ships, sir."

Blacktail gripped his armrests. "Are they Averon ships? Have they spotted us? How many are on an intercept course?"

Barada's ears twitched. "There are no interstellar wakes. Nothing is moving." She turned a few knobs. "There are several large machines in orbit but all appear to be stationary. Nothing coming in or out." She flipped a switch and a machine appeared on the screen. "I don't think it is an Averon ship, sir."

It was ugly. That in itself would have justified Barada's opinion. The ladders, doors and windows looked Chinchillan; although, the structures were devoid of decoration. Then he saw the scale.

"Barada. How big are these creatures?"

"Judging by the size of that ladder and door, the creatures must be 90 mic tall and weigh five thousand zok."

Klaatu's paw shivered as it hovered above the engine controls. "Shall we turn around and run?"

Blacktail shook his head. "Stay on course, half speed." The pup still had stripes in his fur. Ninety mic? He tried to imagine a creature that big. His six mic stature was considered tall and his 100 zok was considered portly. He doubted such a giant would notice stepping on him. He glared in the direction of his computer officer.

"Nikto. What can you tell me about these creatures?"

"They are big, sir."

Through clenched teeth, he spat, "We know that." Blacktail closed his eyes tight and imagined giving Nikto a savage nip. "How high is their technology? Can you translate their language?"

"I am not detecting any high tech power sources. The computers are already working on translation, Captain."

"Good. Let me know when they are finished."

"Finished, sir?" Nikto squeaked.

"Why do you make every conversation so difficult?" he barked. "Yes. Finished."

"It will never finish. The program will refine translation as long as you let it run. The syntax algorithm and the vocabulary tables form multi-indexed contextual-

"Stop!" Blacktail winced at the sharpness of his own voice as it ricocheted off the metal walls. He let out a slow breath and turned to Barada. "Locate a place to land and make contact with one of these creatures."

"I thought that is what you would want." She swiveled away from him to face the large screen on the wall. Her bushy tail curled seductively around her feet. "I've already selected an area with sparse metal structures each containing only one or two large creatures. We will be in synchronous orbit above it in a few tocks." The screen filled with a large rectangular shape. A rainbow colored infrared image of a creature could be seen as if the walls were transparent. Viewed from above and behind, it was not a nice looking creature.

Blacktail glanced around the room. Every eye was fixed on the creature. Klaatu's shivering increased by the moment. "Nikto. Have the translators in the pod in five tocks." His warning glance silenced the first word of his engineer's complaint.

"Are we still going down there?" Klaatu stammered. "They could be predators."

"We are equipped with the most sophisticated weapons ever devised." Blacktail tried to sound confident, but as he looked at the monster, he too felt fear.

"We cannot turn back. We have two hundred tocks to find a solution." He switched the screen to show the planet's large land masses and let that encourage him and the crew for a tock. "I want each of you dressed in your finest military uniform. We will depart in five tocks. Dismissed."

Klaatu's comment weighed heavily on his mind as he walked the multi-colored translucent tube from the control room to his quarters. It was always possible the next alien species would be a predator. Closing the door, he indulged in a scented dust bath before tying the gold ribbon of his pink and yellow captain's bonnet under his chin and checking in the mirror that it was centered between his ears. The tall emerald feather he won from the defeated Averon captain made it even more regal and returned some of his confidence.

Tocks later, the crew was assembled and ready. Even Klaatu looked smart. His simple green and red striped skullcap with a small propeller in the center signified his position. It was not as striking as Barada's headpiece with its twin star-shaped jewels on flexible springs, nor as tall as Nikto's black and white checkered ear-length cone, but it would do.

Nikto passed out communicator earrings and translator pendants. "What is your plan, sir?"

"I hate violence as much as you do," he looked each one in turn. When he looked at Nikto, he couldn't help but wince. "Except for you." He opened a steel box with a thick lid and removed several objects. "We have less than two hundred tocks to find out how this species reacts to aggression. If they are easily intimidated, we will see how they react to diplomacy."

Barada's eyes widened as she looked into the box. "Aren't those Pandora Missiles?" She took a step back. "How far are we prepared to push them?"

Blacktail's face hardened as much as his chubby cheeks would allow. "As far as it takes. Hopefully, we won't have to use the big guns. We'll start with this." He held up a dark green canister with a red button on top. "You all know how to use this; don't you?"

He could see the confusion on their faces. "Come on. There are no stupid questions."

Barada picked up one of the canisters as the rest of the crew shied away. "This is a stench grenade. It makes your eyes water and has a very bad smell. You push the button and roll the canister at your enemy. It releases the gas after five seconds."

"Very good, Barada. How about this?" He handed her a disk that looked like two dinner plates glued together with a thick red material between them.

"That sir, is a terror induction bomb. It makes an ear-piercing noise and throws brightly colored sparks as it spins," she said with trepidation.

Klaatu shivered.

"The horror." Nikto whimpered.

"So, we use the stench grenade first. If the creature is not begging for mercy, we use the terror induction bomb. If it still isn't cowed we will be forced to use a Pandora missile. Are there any other questions?" He looked each in the eye. Even Barada seemed appalled.

Klaatu timidly raised a hand. "Couldn't we try diplomacy first?"

Blacktail's breath caught in his throat. "That is the dumbest thing you have ever said. Enough questions. Let's get on with it." He ushered them into the shuttle. They were silent as the shuttle slid silently toward the surface. It was up to him to make this work. His crew knew their tasks and did them well, but they were not trained soldiers. He closed his eyes and rehearsed what he would say to the giant when it was cowering at his feet.

He felt the final surge as the shuttle flared and settled to a gentle landing. He viewed the not so alien landscape around the shuttle before opening the rear hatch. The lush vegetation made the wild promises of the probe's report seem understated.

"I know you are scared, but this should make you feel better." He patted the shell of the first in a line of transparent spheres. This is the high military achievement of our age. When you are in a transpod, nothing can hurt you. These shells are designed to withstand the weight of ten thousand zok, twice the weight of the creature we will meet. It has motorized weights that allow it to climb steep hills without tiring the driver. Its clear shell allowed for perfect visibility in any direction. All you have to do is walk normally. He loaded the weapons into the holding area in his transpod. Nikto trembled less the moment he closed the transparent door.

The house awaited at the other side of a wide field, framed in a twilight sky. As they got closer the impossible size of the dwelling eroded his confidence. His courage took another hard hit as he came close enough to see into a cage through a window. Inside the cage was an Averon.

At least, its bright feathers certainly made it look like one. Could the giants also be at war with them? The thought of keeping an enemy in a cage seemed unbelievably cruel. He had no translator for Averon and freeing it was not in his mission parameters, but he had to know the truth.

He left the transpod at the base of the wall under the window. It was an easy climb to the ledge. The window was opened at the bottom barely enough to crawl through. The Averon sat motionless with its eyes closed in a filthy cage. Blacktail tapped on the cage lightly at first, then harder.

The bird didn't move until he beat his fists against the bars. It gave no sign it recognized him as an enemy. Clearly, this was not an intelligent creature. Blacktail felt better about turning his back on the creature until it spoke. "Hello," his translator chirped.

Blacktail's heart sank. He could never leave a sentient creature in such a state. It made sense that the Averon would quickly learn the local language. Now that they could communicate, it might give him valuable information. "We will free you. What can you tell us about the giants?"

The Averon turned its back to him. Whether out of distrust or hatred, he could only guess. He scampered down the wall to the others.

"The giant is holding an Averon prisoner. We must free it."

Barada popped the hatch of her transpod and crawled out. "An Averon, here?"

Klaatu was barely audible through the thick glass of his pod. "You want us to help one of them?"

"It may have important intel on the giants." Blacktail looked at the frightened faces of his crew. "Nikto and Barada, go around the house to the left and look for a way in. Klaatu and I will go right. We'll meet on the other side." He climbed into his pod and led the way.

Making his way around the next side of the building, he found a stone path that led to stairs and a door, but the handle was impossibly high. There were also windows far out of reach. They moved on to the next side of the house where they were to meet with the others.

When they grew uncomfortable waiting for Barada and Nikto, Blacktail led Klaatu around the next wall and found empty transpods at the foot of a set of stairs. He breathed easier when he saw Nikto at the top of the stairs gesturing to come see something.

179

Dragging Klaatu by the hand, he climbed the stairs where Barada pushed experimentally prodded a door that was the perfect size for them and their pods. It swung easily from its top hinge.

It was almost too good to be true.

"What do you think uses this door?" Barada whispered. "Are there two intelligent species here? Averons, perhaps?"

Blacktail shook his head. "An Averon entrance would not be on ground level. Let's get the pods up here."

It took a few tocks for them to push the pods to the top of the stairs and the base of the door.

"The Averon is in this corner of the building. The giant could be anywhere. We have one hundred tocks. Let's move out." He rolled his transpod through the door and found himself in a hallway wide enough to be a four lane expressway.

The rest of the crew entered close behind him. The pods rolled silently cushioned by a soft carpet. They hugged the wall which opened into the Averon's room.

"Hello," he greeted them cordially.

"We'll have you out in a second." Blacktail left the safety of his pod and climbed the pole. Lowering himself down on the top of the cage he reached for the simple latch that held the cage closed when he realized the Averon could easily have escaped. Not sure what else to do, he pulled the release and the door sprang open.

The Averon did not bolt but seemed confused and frightened. "Pretty Bird."

"What?" Blacktail tried to make eye contact but the Averon seemed quite agitated.

"What can you tell us about the giants?" he whispered.

"Back in the cage!" it screeched.

"I will try to get you safe passage to any Averon system. We will contact them to come get you."

It whistled loudly then repeated, "Back in the cage."

The noise alone would have alerted the giant. Blacktail hurried back down the pole to the safety of his pod.

"What is wrong with it?" Barada asked.

"I don't know. Has it been tortured to insanity?" He stared up at the cage with her until it began to rain seed shells and poo covered bits of paper.

"Back in the cage," it shrieked.

Blacktail led his crew in a hasty retreat back to the hallway.

Barada rolled next to him. "What now?"

"We go on." He led them to the end of the hallway where the carpet ended at the entrance to a cavernous room with tables, chairs, and metal boxes the size of high rise apartment buildings. Here, the floor was polished planks of wood.

He struck his most confident pose and strode into the room looking for the giant. The transpod clicked loudly in the groves of the wooden floor. A blood chilling low-pitched sound hit him in the stomach. A beast like the fabled zark charged from the shadows. In a second it was on him. He saw the world spin as a paw hit the side of his pod. Fortunately, the stabilizers kept him from feeling the impact as he hit the wall. He wanted to run but terror froze his arms and legs.

The zark hurled a series of sharp barks that turned his blood to ice. Lined with pointed teeth, its mouth was large enough to swallow him whole. The teeth bit against the glass. The pod struggled to maintain its position as the zark's paws hit it from every direction. A low hit sent him flying through the air down the hallway. As he bounced, he steered it as best he could toward the giant door but careened into the pods of his crew which all went spinning in different directions.

Blacktail's military training took over. He opened his hatch and threw a stench grenade as the zark charged down the hallway. It paused to look at the hissing cylinder at its feet, whined and backed away.

From somewhere far away came a new sound. "Fifi!"

The zark turned its head to look.

The floor of the immense building creaked and shook with each slow step of the giant. Blacktail hurried the crew into the room at the end of the hallway where with the insane Averon greeted them loudly. He readied a panic induction bomb as the crew lined up behind him and peered around the corner.

It appeared at the end of the hallway. It was the strangest creature Blacktail had ever seen. It had a mop of hair on its head but its skin was bald. It wore brightly colored cloth over every mic of its body but its face and hands. "What is wrong with you?" The sound of its voice was several octaves lower than a Chinchilla voice. It walked into the cloud of noxious gas and sniffed. It coughed and waved its hand in front of its face. "Bad dog." It turned and disappeared into the far room.

Blacktail checked his crew. His pod weathered the attack without a scratch. He checked the time. He would have to make his decision within 50 tocks. With the weight of his planet pushing him on, he motioned to the crew and stepped forward. His pod protected him from the fumes of the stench grenade that must still fill the hallway.

The giant was seated in the room at the end of the hall with its back to him. The zark looked right at them and backed away. When he was close enough, Blacktail armed the panic bomb and rolled it with expert aim toward the giant. It hit its target and jumped into the air just over the giant's head unleashing its shrill whistling sound and showering the giant in multicolored sparks.

It was a terrifying sight. Blacktail griped the controls of his pod and watched. He could see the terror build as the giant turned and looked up.

Its slow reflexes may have been a result of the immense size of its nervous system. Blacktail readied himself to approach his terror stricken foe.

As the seconds ticked by, Blacktail began to doubt that any nervous system could be this slow. His impatience turned to fear as the giant reached up and let the sparks fall into its hand. It looked positively disappointed when the whistling and sparks stopped. The bomb dropped to the ground exhausted and defeated, exactly like Blacktail's plan.

Blacktail hefted the entire box of Pandora missiles.

"It's hopeless. We have to go back," Nikto whined as his pod rolled next to him.

"What are you going to do?" Klaatu shivered.

"We have to find a way to defeat the monsters or face starvation on our planet." He haphazardly dumped the missiles on the floor and pointed them randomly toward the ceiling. "Take cover," he shouted and slapped each missile's launch button.

He dived into his pod as the first one shot skyward and joined the rest of his crew taking shelter beneath a giant chair. All six were airborne in quick succession. Blacktail covered his ears and closed his eyes tight. Even so, the first flash and concussion set his nerves ablaze and the brightness hurt his eyes. It was all he could do hold his composure through the assault.

The only other time he witnessed the use of this weapon made him glad he saw nothing. The sound alone stunned Averons and Chinchillas alike and the flash caused temporary blindness. It was the cruelest device any Chinchilla had ever devised and only his rigorous training made him callous enough to use it. Even so, he knew he'd eventually feel regret and remorse for what he was forced to do.

He was grateful the transpod protected him from the worst of the noise. Even so, he would be partially deaf for a short time when this was over. Between explosions, he listened for the screams of the giant. The bombardment seemed to last forever. Some part of his brain tried to count the seconds, knowing it would all end in under a tock, but the adrenaline flooding into his system would not allow that much concentration.

His pod swung violently. Blacktail cracked open an eye to see what had caused it and saw a transpod rolling erratically toward another chair. A flash forced him to close his eyes tight.

Then it was over. The monster was on its hands and knees. Gazing at his trembling foe, Blacktail felt strong. Barada's chest was heaving but she seemed fine. Nikto lay curled into a ball at the bottom of his pod. He scanned the room. It wasn't until the giant straightened that he saw Klaatu's pod the in giant's hand.

The giant's mouth moved but only a few words were translated "Are you … the …?"

Blacktail couldn't turn away but watched in fascinated horror as the giant unlatched the hatch of the Klaatu's pod and wrapped his fingers around the helpless crewmember. The giant walked right by the chair the rest of the crew was hiding under. The zark bounced against the giant's leg as if begging for a meal.

Blacktail could only hear the giant as Klaatu begged for his life.

"… you … so cute!" The giant ran one finger along Klaatu's back, seemingly unaware of his pleading.

"Nikto, what is wrong with the translator?"

"Nothing, sir. It has only learned a few words?" Nikto stammered.

Blacktail could not hear Klaatu, but the giant had not done anything but look at him. "It ran for ten tocks and it only learned baby talk?"

"It can speak baby talk in sixty five languages," he said hopefully.

"Multiple languages?" Blacktail yanked and thrashed angrily at the controls. "Why didn't you tell me this?"

Barada cried out. "It can't hear the panic induction bomb or smell the stench grenade. The Pandora hardly phased it. The colony ships haven't got a chance. We have to turn the fleet around."

The giant continued walking to another room carrying Klaatu away. Blacktail was grateful when Klaatu's screams were too far away to be heard.

Blacktail looked at the time. He had ten tocks, not that it mattered. Nikto and Barada were right. It was hopeless." Blacktail pressed a few buttons. "This is Captain Blacktail of the Royal Chinchillan Space Fleet. The planet below is –

"Wait," Nikto cried out.

"Wait for the rest of us to be eaten before we send the message that will prolong thousands of lives?" Blacktail snapped.

"Sir. If you'll allow me to try something."

Blacktail sneered. "What can you do?"

Nikto went running after the giant.

Blacktail shook his head and turned to his only remaining crewmember. "The idiot is going to get himself killed." He pushed a button and continued his recording. "This is Captain Blacktail. The planet is infested with giants. We are hopelessly unable to defeat or defend against them. With deep regret, I –

"Sir?"

"What?" he exploded.

"What if Nikto has a good idea?" she pleaded.

"Listen to yourself. You can't use his name and good idea in the same sentence."

She placed a hand lightly against the glass. "He is giving his life. Shouldn't we at least allow him to try?"

He chided himself for being too fond of the female, but nodded to her. "Very well."

She crept her pod to follow the monster. They hid under a table with full view of the horrific spectacle.

"Another one?" The giant set Nikto and Klaatu on a table.

Klaatu lay twitching at the edge, but Nikto reached toward the giant.

A puzzled look came over the giant who leaned close.

"Hungry," Nikto yelled.

The giant staggered back. "You talk."

Again Nikto gestured and repeated his message into the tiny ear of the giant.

"Hungry? You are hungry? Why didn't you say so?" it opened a cabinet and set several cylinders before the pair. Each cylinder was as tall as they were. The giant put a mound of food on the counter from each container. Each mound would have fed them all for several days.

Nikto nibbled at one then another. "Nuts, Sir. Dried fruit. So much food!" He raised one in each hand. "And it's delicious."

The giant ran its finger down Klaatu's back. "You are so soft," it crooned hypnotically.

Blacktail felt his stomach tighten the giant turned its head. "More …?" He backed away as the giant approached.

Barada steered her pod at the monster's feet and opened the hatch as it reached for her, but the zark came running and reached her first.

"Fifi," the giant warned.

The zark obediently slowed and merely sniffed Barada.

The giant gently lifted Barada and rubbed her against its cheek. "So soft and cute."

Blacktail pressed the delete button and began a new message. "This is Captain Blacktail. The world below you is teeming with willing slaves…

# The Changing Man

**By Brian Goulet**

Brian is currently attending the University of Michigan, where he is taking his final classes for a degree in Journalism and English. He currently works as an editor for Word Branch publishing, but plans on using his degree to work as an editor for one of the Big Five publishers. He is owned by 2 cats.

~~~

*G*randpa, why do the leaves do that?
*Do what?*
*You know...go all red and stuff. Why?*
*Oh, THAT...well, son, I'll tell you what my grandpa told me when I was about your age...*

When the world was young, and all of the people of this Earth singing and dancing, and when they were hungry, they had only to go pluck fruit from the trees. That all changed, though, on the day the Changing Man came. When he first arrived at our people's village, our ancestors thought nothing of it. After all, there were no enemies, and many people traveled for no reason other than the sheer pleasure of it. He was given welcome, and made to feel at home, just as any other traveler would be.

For many days, the man watched our people in silence. He seemed friendly enough, willing to help when help was needed, but he did not go out of his way to make friends, and odd things began happening after his arrival. People would get sick for no reason or have strange accidents. Occasionally, when the fruit was plucked from the trees, it would be sour, or even rotten. The stranger watched all of this with his silent smile.

The man stayed for a full moon's change, what is now called a month, never making friends, rarely speaking, and the whole time strange injuries and illnesses plagued our people. The shaman communed with the gods and told us that the only way to protect our people was to make the man leave. The man, however, having seen how good life was among our people, refused to go. Now, our people did not know violence, for what reason was there to be violent? We had no enemies! But they were afraid. So they forced the man out with sticks and rocks...they made the first weapons. To our eternal shame, they drew the first blood. That is when the Changing Man revealed himself as what he truly was. His features changed; his skin became as white as chalk and his hair as red as the leaves you see on the trees. This man, who had spoken so little, now told our people that it was his nature to bring change wherever he went, and that what we had done, harming one who could not change his own nature, for no other reason than he was different, must be punished. From his fingers fell sparks, and they spread quickly. Nothing the people did could extinguish the flames. They did not kill anybody, for the Changing Man was not a man of violence, but they burned the orchards, every last tree.

From that day on, our people were forced to become nomads, traveling from place to place, just as the Changing Man did, working to feed ourselves. Worse, because of our actions, food was no longer plentiful, but must be carefully worked during the warm months, and packed away against the cold. To this day, the world around us remembers and punishes our people. That is why the leaves turn the red of flame, the red of the Changing Man's hair, and why the world is covered in snow the color of his skin. Pity our ancestors, for because of what they did, the world now suffers the little death of winter.

# Avalon Please Respond

## By Sergio Palumbo

Sergio is an Italian public servant who graduated from Law School working in the public real estate branch. He has published a Fantasy RolePlaying illustrated Manual, WarBlades, of more than 700 pages. Some of his works and short- stories have been published on American Aphelion Webzine, WeirdYear Webzine, YesterYearFiction, AnotheRealm Magazine, Alien Skin Magazine, on Orion's Child Science Fiction and Fantasy Magazine, Farther Stars Than These, on Digital Dragon Magazine, on Kalkion Science Fiction and Fantasy Web Magazine, on Orion's Arm, on Quantum Muse, Surprising Stories, on EMG- ZINE, on The Speculative Edge Magazine, on Australian Antipodean SF, on British Schlock!Webzine , on Australian SQ Mag, and in print inside an American Horror Anthology, title: "Now I Lay Me Down To Reap..." by Sirens Call Publications, inside a British Sci-Fi Anthology, title: "Timeless Worlds" by Schlock Magazine, inside a British Sci-Fi Anthology, title: "Pulpateers" by the same publisher, inside a British Sci-Fi Anthology, title: "The Year's Best Schlock! Sci-Fi 2013" by the same publisher, inside a British Fantasy Anthology, title: "The Year's Best Schlock! Fantasy 2013" by the same publisher, inside a British

Horror Anthology for short- stories, title "TALES OF THE UNDEAD - Hell whore Anthology"… by Horrified Press, inside another British Horror Anthology for short- stories, title "TALES OF THE UNDEAD- Volume II - Hell whore Anthology continues… " by the same publisher, inside a British Sci-Fi Anthology for short- stories, title "JUST ONE MORE STEP Anthology"… by the same publisher , inside another British Sci-Fi Anthology for short- stories, title "DARK IN THE LIMELIGHT"… by the same publisher, inside an American Fantasy Anthology for shorts-stories, title: "Limelight: A Golden Light Anthology" by Chambertonpublishing, inside an American Anthology of Historical/Fantasy shorts-stories by the same publisher, too, title: "Gaslight: A Golden Light Anthology", inside an American Horror Anthology for short- stories, title "Dark Light 2" by Crushing Hearts Black Butterfly Publishing, inside an American Horror Anthology for short- stories, title "Cirque d'Obscure" by the same publisher, inside an American Horror Anthology, title: "Temptations and other sins" by Fantastic Horror Press, inside an American Anthology of Urban Fantasy/Horror shorts-stories, title: "Blood and Guts: An Anthology of the Gross and Disgusting" by Static Movement Publications, inside an American Horror/Steampunk Anthology for shorts-stories, title: "Dreadful Legacies" by the same publisher, inside a Fantasy/Sci-Fi Anthology for shorts-stories, title: "LocoThology 2013: Tales of Fantasy & Science Fiction- Volume 3" by Loconeal Publishing, inside a Horror Anthology for shorts-stories, title: " Undead Living" by Sunbury Press, and inside a new American Horror Anthology, title: "Mental Ward: Stories from the Asylum..." by Sirens Call Publications, inside an American Horror Anthology, title: "Slaughter House: The Serial Killer Edition - Volume 2", by the same publisher, inside an Australian Sci-Fi Anthology, title: "Star Quake 1- Best of SQ Mag's 2012"- Anthology, inside a CanadianHorror Anthology, title: "Blood and Roses" by Scarlett River Press, inside an Urban Fantasy/Horror Anthology for shorts-stories, title: "Miseria's Chorale" by Forgotten Tomb Press, inside an American Anthology of Horror shorts-stories, title: "Deadhead miles" by Spook Show Publishing, inside a new British Horror Anthology, title "Night Shade- Volume I... " by Little Bird Publishing, inside another American Horror Anthology, title "The Dead walk" by Breaking Fate Publishing and will appear soon, in print, inside anAmerican Horror Anthology for short- stories, title "Dark Light 4" by Crushing Hearts Black Butterfly Publishing, in another Canadian Horror Anthology, title: "Tortured Souls Volume 1" by Scarlett River Press, inside an American Sci-Fi Anthology for short-stories, title "Out of Phase: Tales of Sci-Fi Horror" by Sirens Call Publications, inside an American Anthology for short- stories, title "Automaton: A Steampunk Anthology" by Baird Speculative Fiction, inside a British Horror Anthology for short- stories, title "PLAGUE..." by Horrified Press, inside another British Horror Anthology for short- stories, title "TALES OF THE UNDEAD - Hell whore III Anthology... " , by the same publisher, inside another AmericanSteampunk/Horror Anthology, title: "Steampunk Monster Hunter - The Dark Monocle" by Emby Press, inside a British Urban Fantasy/Horror Anthology for short- stories, title "Cursed Curiosi-ties..." by Barbwire Butterfly Books , inside another British Urban Fantasy/Horror Anthology for short- stories, title "Sweet Dreams & Night Terrors..." by Silent Fray Productions , inside another British Horror Anthology for short- stories, title "Undercurrents of Fear..." by the same publisher, in another American Anthology for Fantasy short-stories, title "Hidden in Your World" by Visionary Press, inside an American Paranormal Anthology for short- stories, title "Bloody Sexy" by Hot Ink Press, inside another British Steampunk Anthology for short- stories, title "Steamworld..." by Thirteen Press, inside an

192

American Anthology of Horror shorts-stories, title: " Demonology" , by Static Movement Publications, inside an American Anthology of Fantasy/Horror shorts-stories of strictly lesbian and bisexual female tales, title: "Magickally Delicious" by the same publisher and then inside an American Anthology of Horror shorts-stories by the same publisher, again, title: "Love at first bite" '

He is also a scale modeler who likes mostly Science Fiction and Real Space models, some of his little Dioramas have been shown also on some Italian (scale model) magazines like Soldatini, Model Time, TuttoSoldatini and online on American site StarShipModeler, MechaModelComp, on British SFM: UK site and Italian SMF .

Some Sci-Fi/fantasy/Horror short- stories by him in Italian have been published on Alpha Aleph, Alpha Aleph Extra, Algenib, Oltre il Futuro, Nugae 2.0, SogniHorror, La Zona Morta, edizioni Lo Scudo, Antologia Robot ITA 0.1, Antologia Il Segreto dell'Universo, Antologia E-Heroes, etc.'

The internet site of his Model Club "La Centuria": www.lacenturia.it

~~~

"Through the darkness, the light comes…
but it's only the ray of a laser rifle
fired in the middle of the battle,
not a light of hope, you know…"

Unknown Space Royal Marine's quote

Having exited the main hall, Frank Stephens hurriedly entered the room that he had been ordered to go into that morning as soon as the doors opened wide. His chestnut eyes, the same color as his hair, were subdued, but his senses were always ready to respond to anything that might happen. This ability was mainly due to the long, intensive training that he had undergone for ten years, which had finally turned him into the man he was now. Frank was a notable and valuable soldier, 37-years-old, and was the leader of a team of Space Royal Marines from the powerful Earth Kingdom. His rank was something that few in the Military could accomplish, of course. Slender but well-muscled, very intelligent and experienced, Frank wasn't the kind of person who easily lost his power of concentration before some unexpected or terrible event - in fact men at arms like him were not approached to do some easy task or for any duty that a common officer could do.

The young man's eyes briefly lingered on the roof, the floor, the windows and the many details that came to his mind: he really wanted to have a clear picture of that place. The azure-greenish uniform he presently wore consisted of an 'A' and 'B' part as modern tradition required. Unlike the Dress Blues of a time gone by, this one was not authorized to be worn during leave and liberty wear. For example, the trousers weren't allowed with either the long-sleeved or the short-sleeved battleground shirt: this outfit was only permitted for enlisted personnel during ceremonies, social events or very important briefings, if provided by the command structure. This occasion was the last of those choices.

Once inside, he was introduced by a tall, middle-aged general named Bretts to another man, a skinny blonde, dark-eyed scientist, called

Andrews. The man of science was in his early forties, a plain gray civilian attire on, and appeared to be at least a foot shorter than Frank: he was already sitting next to the main wooden desk of the high ranking officer. There was not much time for formalities, apparently, as the briefing began almost immediately.

"Did you ever hear of Avalon Station, Captain Stephens?" the general asked Frank as he sat and the doors of the spacious windowless room hissed closed behind him. The man scratched at his bristly beard, which was offset by his attentive light blue eyes.

There was a brief silence as the short-haired captain who wore the orange insignia of his famous corps tried to remember the name. Finally he visibly nodded. "Yes, I do remember it, Sir. It's that small advanced space station Earth Kingdom built some months ago, positioning it at the farthest point in our galaxy as an up-to-date science lab meant to keep intense observation of the intergalactic gap. That's right, isn't it?"

"Correct!" the general stated. "Well, it disappeared one week ago, along with everyone of its restricted crew who provided the station with the small amount of human help that it needed, given the high technology it was provided with. But this information is top secret, Captain; of course you can understand why."

"Indeed!" Frank burst out in a fierce voice. Then he dared to ask something. "And, Sir, if I am allowed to know, how did it happen? Who destroyed it?"

"Actually, Captain, it has not been destroyed, not at all. It seems to have been positioned elsewhere, and is now just outside our galaxy, precisely in the direction of Sculptor Dwarf Galaxy. This is an unusual position because it is very far away from any other inhabited world or known star, as a matter of fact."

'Positioned elsewhere?' the Captain considered those words in his mind, in silence. "How is it possible, Sir?" he finally asked. "I mean…why is it there? There's nothing out there, in such a wide portion of empty space…"

"Almost nothing!" the scientist sitting next to him said. "There's mainly gas out there, but even gas is something. There are countless baryons - composite subatomic particles belonging to the hadron family - which occupy the enormous distances between galaxies. These are very difficult to spot and examine, certainly, as they mainly represent some very diffuse gases in space which are also called 'whim': short for 'warm-hot intergalactic medium'. Commonly only the coldest part of such structures are really seen and studied, because those are more abundant than anything else."

"But, the question still remains. How did the station get to that position? Who put it there?"

"We don't know!"

Andrews simply opened his mouth in disbelief.

There was a long pause, and then the general started talking in a low tone, raising both his vivid eyes to meet the Captain's. "In reality, we think that Avalon Station has been stolen… And probably the ones who did it, using whatever strange technology they possess, want the station's creators, that is Mankind itself, to come and try to get it back, sooner or later. Our politicians consider it a sort of unspoken invitation to go there, a way to discover if we are really able to travel that far."

After some surprise, Frank stared at the two others who were there. They didn't say anything and appeared to be waiting for him to ask more questions about that delicate, secret matter. "And are we, Sir? – able to travel that far, I mean?" the captain eventually pointed out.

General Bretts turned his face towards Andrews, and then he slightly smiled and nodded. "Yes, probably we are…but the travel involves many dangers, obviously."

Frank made a strange expression, and then he finally understood why he had been called to the meeting and why he was there. 'When there's a danger, send in the Royal Space Marines, of course…' Visibly frowning, the Captain asked: "Do you plan to despatch a military team of mine there, Sir?"

The general scratched at his beard again before pointing towards the officer. "A science research team, meant to work in connection with the Military, would be better, I think. And you and your well-trained men will be part of it, clearly."

"Clearly, Sir" Frank replied. "How long before we move out, Sir?"

"It will be soon, very soon…" the other stated.

'Very short notice, but what's new about that?' the Captain considered. 'And for the longest trip in space that any man has ever tried up till now…'

\*\*\*\*\*

The strange mission was on track within two days, even though Captain Stephens couldn't call it a recovery mission, as they wouldn't be able to really bring Avalon Station back to their galaxy once they got there. Nor were they sure that reaching that area of space was their final destination, in reality…

The starting point was the last known star within the farthest arm of the galaxy the humans lived in. Beyond that lay a huge lifeless ice planet orbiting the star itself where the Earth Kingdom Army had built two outposts in order to patrol the extreme outer limits of where men had been able to reach and keep solar systems under their control. The planet was also a source for many uncommon minerals and expensive crystals that several mining companies excavated in the mountain ranges - which were also the key elements in the assembling of arms and engines made for many special purposes.

How strange that such a feeble, almost forgotten luminous point and the neglected iced planet void of any living creatures, except a few workers from other worlds, would witness the first - and hopefully successful - try of Mankind to finally travel out beyond the galaxy that had seen the birth and rise of the human species millions of years ago. That star system was situated right before the empty darkness that stretched past the thousands and thousands of massive bodies behind it, in a sort of unpredictable passage from the land of lights - if you wanted to call it that. The humans already knew very well that the space beyond that star system was made up only of that black, silent and almost endless expanse full of nothing. No starry sky from that point on. Nothing at all.

Certainly their galaxy was very wide-ranging - so magnificent that a holo-screen shot of it with high-resolution colours might be a wonderful sight to every sentient species, undoubtedly. Nonetheless, it wasn't just a specific location within that sea of stars that they wished to get to at present.

Intergalactic spaces were incredibly huge, physical gaps filled with a tenuous gas of very low average density. Although that gas was very warm by terrestrial standards, a lot of computer simulations and observations indicated that up to half of the atomic matter of the whole of reality just might exist in this rarefied state. A very strange thing, if you just personally thought of it...Sensitive surveys had been made of several forms of hot and cold gas in the intergalactic space outside clusters of galaxies and a few indications were that, long ago, there were once vast clouds, but humans didn't know where those clouds went because they could no longer be detected, except as 'absorption features' in the light from very distant bodies.

It was believed that many if not all of these clouds were ultimately 'eaten' by other galaxies. At times, stars could get pulled away from their positions during collisions between galaxies and these could end up in intergalactic space as lonely bodies. Some researchers had previously detected those intergalactic wanderers, too. In some cases an entire population of such 'stellar outcasts', as somebody had named them, had been spotted here and there across the sky. Astronomers had long been trying to calculate exactly how many of these stars might be present, but it seemed from the level of optical background light that their numbers were rather small. Anyway, nothing like this stood between their massive galaxy and the near gravitationally bound system called Sculptor Dwarf - the scientists who had researched and planned their mission were sure about it.

Galaxies had been historically categorized according to their apparent shape, usually referred to as their visual morphology. The Sculptor Dwarf Galaxy was merely a faint dwarf spheroidal structure, discovered in 1937 by Harlow Shapley - an American astronomer who died in 1972, more than four hundred years ago. It turned out that this Dwarf Galaxy was just a small satellite of the Milky Way. Moreover, it contained only 4 percent of the heavy elements that made up Mankind's galaxy, making it similar to primitive and very old structures seen at the edge of the observable sky.

In order to reach such a distant part of space, which was just past the border of the cosmic area that humans lived within, you had to make several quantum-jumps from one point to another and then set the instruments to accomplish the longest quantum-jump from that last location of inhabited space to the destination you wanted to get to. Of course, any jump had a maximum range available, especially if you had to move through the many stars and planets that filled the galaxy itself -

but you could try to spin your spaceship a bit further away if you were travelling outside of the galactic boundary. But even when doing this, there was a maximum distance you were allowed to reach in the end, as other problems and difficulties happened...

As a matter of fact, the modern technology of quantum-jump travel was limited because of the gravity implications of the stars, planets and rocks being in space that you were moving through at a faster-than-light speed. You didn't want to appear again and stumble into an unknown body or an obstacle while travelling at that rate, certainly, which result would be only destruction and death. After all, such jumps made use of gravity itself, generated from a huge body at the starting point, and transformed it into a sort of perfect energy to move the space vehicle over vast distances.

The fact was that, exactly because of this reason, as you reached the end of the stars that were at the boundary of the galaxy, you didn't have anything else huge enough around to rely upon in order to accomplish more than a single quantum-jump. This was why no one had ever been able to explore the wide gaps between galaxies so far. Other than that, such conglomerations of stars continued to move away from each other more and more - because of dark matter and dark energy whose effects and real consistency were still pretty much unknown - so they would be situated at an increasing distances with the passing of time. Ultimately, the day would come when one single galactic body would stand as a lonely island made up of many lights without anything else around, being surrounded only by complete darkness and an incredibly empty space forever when all the others galaxies appeared to be lost objects. Of course, a lot of time still had to pass before all that happened.

Anyway, Avalon Station had been spotted at a specific point that stood at a distance of two long-range jumps, and that meant that some technological innovation had to be used if human beings wanted to reach it. Andrews was one of the more brilliant scientists from Earth Kingdom and he had some modern devices at his disposal so that he could help them do their duty. A new machine, capable of collecting and storing gravity energy in order to use it to spin a spaceship for more than a single quantum-jump, had been built for experiments some years ago, but nobody had ever tried to put it into practice for such a long journey until today, as the danger involved was really too great. What if the device itself broke once the jump had been completed, when the space-vehicle was already far away from the galaxy boundary and there was no other way to repair it and get back? That was a very good question, still unanswered. And what if you had some problems requiring immediate assistance from another ship, at the time you had already reached a point in deep space where no one else could get to you, in order to help you or your crewmembers? That was another interesting argument, undoubtedly.

Despite all these doubts about the journey, Headquarters had decided to let them go. The need to discover what had really happened to Avalon Station was too important, apparently, and a crew of scientists and military troopers seemed to be expendable, anyway… As a matter of fact, a Royal Space Marine went wherever he was ordered to, every single time a need arose, without questioning his orders.

And then the real travel had to begin, in order to reach the farthest point in space that humans had ever experienced! From that point the jump would be made into the unknown. Captain Frank wasn't sure they would really get there, or that they would ever be able to make it back according to what had been decided by the high ranking officers, but he and his men were there to get the job done, and they would give it their best try - as usual.

"One hour before the first quantum-jump outside our galaxy," a voice resounded across the whole control room of the spaceship. As the man heard the enormous engines begin to warm up, a strange sensation filled his mind. Then he noticed the great anxiety on the face of Andrews, the scientist next to him, and he thought that there was someone else that had even more fear and worry than he did.

'I've never traveled so far away from all the other stars and planets before. The blackness of that unending, empty space stretching out there makes me feel uneasy, and that has never happened to me before,' the captain told himself. 'But probably no one else had ever gone so far. There's always a first time...'

Their transport, the Small Terrapin, was a very long reddish spacecraft - the shape of a winged turtle with a very long tail - capable of extraordinary performance, thanks to its twin boosters. Its Quantum drive allowed travel across unthinkable distances in space. The wide tail was full of many sensors and they were very useful for discovering any unusual objects around the ship.

The jolt as the spaceship departed from the mooring duct was considerably harder than he remembered from the past, but this was to be expected as the means of transport they were aboard was really a very powerful one. And it had to be so if it was going to reach that point that stood in the middle of nothing. The same nothing they were going to get to very soon, if they didn't all end up dying in the process, of course...

*****

The spacecraft disappeared and materialized again with all the crewmembers regaining consciousness eventually. As soon as they were able to, the ones aboard walked the metallic floors, did their jobs and completed the routine tests before allowing the green light to slow navigation in space.

Looking through the reinforced window, along the yellowish, metallic bulkhead of the room, Andrews considered how small the partly elongated/partly tubular Avalon Station appeared now. It was in the middle of that seemingly endless black space they had just reached after their insidious travel across such a huge distance that no human had ever gone before. But they had made it, finally!

There were no stars out there, no planets or rocks - at least as none had been detected by humans. And their instruments seemed to give a clear confirmation of it all, without a doubt. Such an emptiness, that uncommon expanse made up of darkness, was something that could easily overwhelm your senses and finally get the better of you. You had to really prove able to be sitting still and taking no notice in order to not faint before such an unusual wonder, by remaining indifferent to all that strangeness, no matter how wise, old or experienced you were. In their case, and specifically speaking about such an unknown area of space, humans couldn't imagine what lay within those dark boundaries. Maybe there was something really valuable in that area. Or perhaps there was just something very dangerous and deadly.

"Avalon Station, please respond…Avalon, please respond…" the Royal Space Marine at the interplanetary radio kept asking again and again. They had started their attempt at communication with the control room of the station when they had completed their second quantum-jump, but with no result. Whatever had happened to that place, it seemed that its crew - who were aboard it at the time it had suddenly disappeared – was unable to respond to their call or they were already dead. 'Who knows what they experienced…' the scientist told himself.

"Avalon Station, please respond…" the litany went on another time, but things remained the same. At least all the systems seemed to be functioning well, and the course appeared calm and without any disturbances so far. While checking the instrumentation again, the young man in the uniform with a strong build shook his head in dejection; he then turned to the Captain, ready to receive his new orders.

"Alright, soldiers!" Frank Stephens stated, tidying his spacesuit up. "We can't get any reply from the inside. Be ready, check all of your equipment and prepare to board the station ten minutes from now."

The six Royal Space Marines did as ordered and they lined up along the floor before entering the small armed spacepod that was meant to bring them all to their destination. As they were inside sitting on the sturdy seats positioned along both sides, Frank looked at the portable detecting device that he held with both hands, and then made an announcement to the others. "My data indicates that some movements have just been detected a moment ago on the space station. So, there's somebody, or something alive on the station. Be ready for whatever it is!"

The eyes of the scientist looked amused and very attentive. The captain noticed it at once, and that worried him a bit, as a matter of fact. "You'd better stay in the spaceship and wait for our return," Frank suggested in a low tone.

"No way! If there are intelligent, alien beings inside the station now, I wouldn't pass up such an opportunity to meet them for any reason."

The captain stared at Andrews for a moment, considering his interest and why they all had come that long way, so he nodded in the end. "Alright…but just stay with me, I want you to always stay behind me! It is safer…"

"Please, make way!" the scientist said, cutting it short and making a wide gesture to the Captain. Frank gave the orders and the team of Space Royal Marines moved out, surrounding the two and getting ready to disembark.

Landing didn't prove difficult, nor was there anything insidious revealed with the opening of the hatch into the Avalon. As soon as their small spacepod was docked and stopped, the soldiers walked quickly across the cargo bay of the station. While they were deployed around, standard issue weapon at hand, and were working their way to the upper level where the control room was, many worries were on their mind, even though their overall features didn't show any fear. Just a single glimpse of danger or an unexpected problem at a corner or a hallway had to be properly evaluated and dealt with before it was too late. If it wasn't handled immediately, the consequences would be of great significance for the whole team clearly.

The route to the heart of the station proved to be easy, not a single bad thing happened; nothing impeded their movements along the way. But it was when they reached the control room itself that they finally saw before their own eyes that strange, incredible situation that no one would have ever expected to discover in there.

A group of thirty bipedal robot-like mechanisms, each being much taller than two men in height, and broader than the back of a modern altitude-auto - wider than 18 feet... - stood in the middle of the bulbous open room surrounded by hundreds of videos, instruments and equipped seats that made up the control room of Avalon Station itself. Their round metallic heads displayed highly capable optics for precision tasks (maybe also targeting, the captain considered...) and their hand design maximized potential small-arms use, or at least that was what Frank immediately was afraid of. After all, it was part of his training...

Their bodies appeared to be very strong and had some front storage compartments, likely meant for tools or provisions, while every leg was bulky and slender at the same time, giving them all an increased, tactical mobility, certainly. With armor plating that was almost completely gray in color, they seemed to be models ready to be deployed on many different kinds of terrain, maybe also extra-vehicular activity, or even directly into space.

But there was something that surprised the captain, a detail that frightened him most of all: those unknown constructs appeared to be in wait, probably just waiting for them to arrive, though it was incredible that such a thing could be happening now!

"Welcome!" the robot-like face of the first one said. He stood in front of all the others in the group and posed as their leader.

"Who are you and what are you doing in here?" Captain Stephens asked the unusual mechanism, keeping his hands positioned on his short-range rifle, ready to fire against his opponent if the necessity arose, certainly.

"You can call us LK 9, and we are pleased to meet you on this space station of yours."

"So, you do know that this place is property of Earth Kingdom?" It was the scientist who was speaking now. "Why did you bring it here, and more than that, how did you do it? And where is its crew now?"

"We're here to respond to all of your questions, of course."

"That is very kind of you..." Frank said in a wary tone. "But it probably would have been nicer if you hadn't taken the Avalon Station in the first place. Don't you agree?"

"It would have been more polite, but if we had left things alone, our end would not have been achieved," the mechanism replied.

"And what is that end exactly?"

"From the energy signals we received from all the colonies you built in your galaxy, we knew you could travel this far, so we decided to take your new space station out of its position..."

"Why? For what purpose?" Andrews asked the robot at once. "And who are you?"

"We did it in order to force you to come here." It was a plain answer, whatever it meant.

"Did you want to meet us in person? Why didn't you reach one of the worlds within our kingdom? That seems to be unlikely, anyway...Are you unable to enter our galaxy for some reason? Did you have some problem with that, maybe?"

"No, actually..." the robot replied. "The species of our Masters – by the way, they call themselves The Strong People- is 4 million-years-old, so they are much older than your species and far more evolved than you are, of course. But they are afraid that one day in the foreseeable future your species might reach the galaxy where they live, which is the one you commonly call the Sculptor Dwarf Galaxy, being about 290,000 light-years away from the space sector where you are standing now. So, that's why we are here, on behalf of them all, ready to execute their orders as usual."

"What orders?" a suspicious Frank asked the other, without releasing the grip on his reliable weapon.

"We were sent here just to discover if your technology could represent a threat to their existence. Better: in order to know if you were able to travel across the wide gaps that separate galaxies in space. We stole this station of yours and just remained aboard waiting for your next move. We hadn't detected any of your vessels travelling outside of your galaxy before, but we supposed that you could succeed it if you really wanted to. Your technology level was high enough to make sure you got here, if you just went to the extremes and if you were forced to do so, but we had to be certain before doing our duty..."

"That being?" the scientist insisted in a decisive voice that requested respect, despite the much bigger size of the robots themselves that looked down on him.

"He's right...Make your intentions plain!" the captain said.

"Reaching this place between two galaxies is just like a sort of test, someone passes it and someone else fails. And all the species that fail survive in the end…" the voice of the metallic mouth was calm and reasonable. But the complete coldness you could sense in it was not less troublesome than a sudden unwanted break along the mooring duct attached to the ship they had just been walking through, whose terrible sound made everyone immediately understand that air was seeping out into open space at a very fast rate. It was obvious that in a matter of seconds the humans were going to face some very drastic consequences.

As a sense of bewilderment and fear started appearing on the faces of all the humans in that bulbous control room, the one who was clearly the leader of the robot team stated the obvious. "The fact that you proved to be capable of getting here reveals that you are going to become a dangerous opponent in a matter of a few centuries. So, there is no alternative for us. Now, if you don't mind, we have a job to do on behalf of our Masters, before heading into your galaxy and exterminating all the other members of your species…"

And that being said, many colorful rays were fired from the retractable, translucent hands of the robots and the bloodshed began. Some of the Royal Space Marines tried to defend themselves and return the shots, the Captain himself included, but they seemed to be very slow in comparison to the alien mechanisms, so they soon started falling to the ground, dropping dead.

"They had evolved too much…" the robotic leader said when it was all over and no human still moved or cried out because of their wounds, except one.

"Or maybe not enough, in comparison to our powerful older Masters…" another mechanism of the team added, his voice as cold as a piece of steel. The first one nodded, then he ordered the others to seize the only surviving human, which was a bruised Andrews, lying not far from the corpse of the Captain.

"Let's start testing the body of this man according to the instructions we received. At first, we'll have the more painful experiments done on him, then we'll try to discover what illnesses can easily affect his tissues, and so we'll determine the best weapon to be used against the humans. Soon all this information will be finally at our Master's' disposal, and our plan will be ready to be deployed in its entirety."

The robots did as requested without worrying too much about the aching feeble Andrews that they were forcibly and painfully moving around the control room in order to get to the labs below.

"Another easy win for our revered Masters, as usual, after all…"

*The End . . . for now*

# About the Anthology

The Word Branch Publishing Science Fiction Anthology is the result of an annual contest open to writers around the world. All profits go toward a literacy charity chosen on the basis of need and reach. Everyone involved with the project—editors, writers, the illustrator, and technical support—donate their time and resources to make the project a success.

This year's chosen literacy charity is The Kentucky Reading Association. The Kentucky Reading Association is a professional organization of educators and individuals actively engaged in the development of literacy throughout the Commonwealth. They are committed to encouraging lifelong reading for pleasure and learning, providing information related to literacy, increasing opportunities for professional growth, and promoting research-based instructional practices. http://www.kyreading.org/

As a thank you for supporting these writers and our literacy cause, we would like to offer readers a 10% discount off all book purchases from Word Branch Publishing. Enter the code CD10 at checkout.

To see more titles like this one, go to Word Branch Publishing's online book shop: https://www.wordbranch.com/book-shop.html

Word Branch is an independent publishing company located in the heart of Appalachia.  We represent talented new and emerging authors who need a venue to make their voices heard.  We offer unique titles in both paperback and e-books in a variety of genres including science fiction, fantasy, young adult, and spiritual.

https://www.wordbranch.com/